Where Do We Go From Here

Jae Henderson & Mario D. King

Where Do We Go From Here

Printed in the United States

Put It In Writing
274 North Parkway
Memphis, TN 38105

Foreword

This book grew out of a desire for two people to work together to better our black community. To do this, we have to look at many things one of which is our black families and relationships. What better way to show how we are weakening the structure of our homes and our communities than to illustrate it in a story.

In 2014, a startling statistic was released that 72% of African American babies are born to unwed mothers. Some of those were unplanned pregnancies that occurred because two individuals merely found one another physically attractive. There was no relationship, no commitment and no foundation.

Nothing that lasts is built without a strong foundation and that includes our black families. According to a 2014 article released in the *Washington Post* children from two-parent households tend to be more successful at school, work and in their marriages. There are several factors that contribute to this but the one that most resonated with Marcus and myself is that children with married parents have more engaged parents, which means they have more time to spend with them to teach them, monitor them, encourage them, nurture them, love them, etc.

It would be foolish to think that we could stop unmarried people from having sex but perhaps we could encourage people to use protection and realize the importance of marriage and family before creating life. Sex is more than recreation. It's a responsibility that could end up impacting more than just the two people engaging in it.

This is only beginning, Jae Henderson and Mario D. King hope to hold events that uplift, encourage and enlighten but what better place for two authors to begin than in a book. We hope you enjoy the story of Natalie and Marcus. Yet, more importantly we hope you receive the message imparted within it.

Jae & Mario

Chapter 1

WHERE DO WE GO FROM HERE?

Natalie and Marcus stared silently at the white plastic stick on the vanity. It seemed like the longest few minutes of their lives, and when the plus sign appeared in the small results window, they both were in a state of disbelief. Neither one knew what to say. This wasn't supposed to happen. They weren't a couple. They could best be described as "friends with benefits." This wasn't the way Natalie wanted to usher in motherhood. She planned on being married to a man she loved, financially secure and prepared mentally and emotionally to take on the challenge of being responsible for another person's well-being. Marcus was a great guy, but he wasn't her boyfriend. If he wanted a relationship with her, she would have no problem with it, but he had made it clear that although he thought she was cool, he wasn't interested in having a girlfriend right now. She didn't see the need to force the issue. He came to see her regularly. He was kind to her, and they had AMAZING sex! It was almost like he was her boyfriend. However, this put their arrangement in a different light.

They both continued to stand there silently for a few more minutes. Natalie was the first to break the silence, but what she said was far from profound. "Wow!"

Marcus countered with, "Damn!"

"I know we didn't plan this, but please don't ask me to have an abortion. I can't kill my baby," said Natalie in a soft and somber voice.

Marcus continued to stare intently at the pregnancy test as if the results would change if he looked at it long enough or hard enough. "OK," he said.

Natalie finally broke her gaze from the vanity and directed it at her lover. "That's all you have to say?"

Marcus looked into Natalie's pleading eyes. He knew she needed him to say something positive. To tell her everything was going to be fine, but he wasn't sure that was true. She was a nice enough person, but he didn't want a kid with her. He planned to have all of his children with his wife, and she certainly wasn't someone he would marry. She had a bangin' body and a magical mouth, and that's what kept him coming to see her. Not to mention the fact that she made him feel like a king, waiting on him hand and foot. She seemed to get enjoyment from pleasing him, and who was he to deny her happiness? Beyond that, he didn't really have a reason for spending time with her. She stimulated him sexually but not intellectually. All she seemed to care about was celebrity gossip and her dog, Pepper. How did this happen? They had been careful. He always used a condom . . . except for that one time when they were in the park and then climbed in the back of his Explorer a few weeks ago and that time when they were in a restaurant and went to the bathroom for a quickie and that time last week. Well maybe they weren't that careful.

"I don't know what to say. This is serious," said Marcus.

Natalie looked at him in disgust. "Thanks, Einstein. I never would have figured that out. How do you feel about this?"

Marcus suddenly felt like there was a morbidly obese man standing on his chest while eating a turkey leg. Natalie's bathroom had always been small, but at that moment, it felt miniscule. Why was she asking him all these questions? Did she really expect him to answer?

"Marcus, I need to know what we're going to do about this. Where do we go from here?"

We? We? As in the TWO of us? There is NO two of us. There is only me, Marcus. The guy that could come over here and have my sexual needs attended to at any time, and then there's you, the good girl closet freak who was willing to give it to me. I never took you around my friends. You only met my mother because she dropped by without an invitation. The most we've done is go to the movies and get something to eat. There is NO we.

Those words ran through Marcus's mind, but what escaped his lips was, "Are you sure it's mine?"

Natalie sat down on the toilet. Marcus had no idea how she felt about him. She always knew if she shared it she would lose him. Some women would be happy to be able to have a child to keep a guy like him around, but she wasn't. She felt like she hit the jackpot when he asked for her number. She had never been with a guy that fine before. She wanted him to be in her life because he loved her, and then their child could be a by-product of that love. He was the only man she wanted and the only man she had slept with in the last year. She figured because he was always coming over he must like her too. He even took her out from time to time, but it was always back to her place or his for some extracurricular activities, but she didn't mind because in that department, he was the MVP.

"Of course, it's yours. I haven't been with anyone but you. We agreed to be monogamous, remember?"

Marcus could tell that he hurt her feelings, but he had to ask. He was being a jerk. He felt the overwhelming need to leave. "I have to go, Natalie."

She looked at him with pleading eyes once again. "Do you have to? I feel like we should talk this out or something." What she wanted to say was I need you to hold me because I'm scared. She wrapped her arms around herself and began to rock back and forth. She wanted to cry, but she didn't. Not in front of Marcus. She would not use tears to make him stay.

Marcus wasn't a bad guy. He wanted to soothe Natalie's fears, but he also didn't want to lie to her. He had done his best not to do that for the past three months. She said she understood their arrangement, and she was fine with them having sex with no commitment. Her only requirement was that he didn't sleep with other people. He didn't mind because he really wasn't that kind of guy and she knew how to hold his attention. But this changed everything. It was no longer just fun and sex. He didn't have to be at work for a few hours, but he wanted to be anywhere but there in that bathroom looking at that stupid test. "I'll call you later," he said.

"Sure," responded Natalie. She ended their conversation with her usual, "Be safe."

"Thanks. You too."

Marcus reached out his hand and touched her shoulder. It was the only reassuring gesture he could muster at the moment. It was cold and hard. She usually felt warm and receiving of him. Natalie continued to rock herself back and forth. She didn't even look at him. His hand felt as cold as his response to this life-altering news. She watched his back as he walked out of the bathroom. They were about to bring a life into this world. Shouldn't there be a little joy somewhere? She listened to his footsteps as Marcus made his way down the steps and out her front door. Only then did she release the tears she was holding hostage. The last thing she wanted was a baby with a man who didn't want her. Pepper, her Yorkshire terrier, came in the bathroom, leapt into her lap, and licked her cheek. At least someone cared about her.

Chapter 2

MARCUS

I guess you can say I had a severe case of the *Mondays*. I spent the entire weekend preparing for an important client meeting. This meeting was going to make or break our third-quarter performance. I had to get my head back in the game so I spent the last 45 minutes to an hour sitting in my car with a cluster of thoughts. I was better but not good. Kristine, one of my colleagues, recognized that I was not my usual self as I entered the building where I worked. As soon as I entered my office, my coffee was awaiting me—the usual, no sugar nor cream. I shuffled through my portfolio to be sure I had everything I needed. As I began to look over my notes, I heard two subtle knocks at the door. Before I could say "come in," Kristine sashayed across the room and took a seat. I've never dated outside of my race, but I always told myself and a few friends, if I ever did—Kristine would be a great place to start. I caught a whiff of her usual perfume of choice, Chanel No. 5. Classic and captivating. I've always been somewhat of a sucker for the beautiful scent of a woman. To be honest, that is what initially attracted me to Natalie.

As Kristine removed a manila folder from her leather satchel, she asked me, "Is everything okay this morning?"

I nodded slightly and replied, "I'll admit, I'm a little flustered, but it's nothing that will distract me from the meeting. We need to close this deal, and trust me, I know neither of us wants those sticks in the home office breathing down our necks for the next quarter."

As I began to gather my thoughts, I saw Stephanie, our receptionist, walk past my window. Normally, I wouldn't have paid too much attention, but this day was different. Stephanie was seven months pregnant, and I immediately began to think about Natalie and our current situation. Kristine must have noticed the sudden change in my demeanor.

"Are you sure everything is all right? If you need me to run—"

I cut her off immediately and replied, "I *can* and *will* run the meeting. You just be sure to highlight the fluctuating market and how our product will minimize seasonal declines." She didn't put up a fight, she just replied, "Well, consider this deal closed, Mr. Colbert."

I smiled and replied, "That's Mr. Marcus J. Colbert." We shared a laugh from the inside joke. However, similar to the tears of a clown . . . my facial expression was insinuating one thing, but my inner soul was torn.

Later that evening, I decided to indulge in some major me-time. No friends, no family, no Natalie, and most importantly—no work. I just wanted it to be me and my thoughts. The only company I needed was my good ol' friend, Jack. I ended up at one of Nashville's premiere spots, Red Carpet Bar & Lounge. It was a typical Monday night there. There were plenty of distractions that normally would have caught my attention. However, my mind was, all of a sudden, looking past distractions and narrowing toward the future. You see, I've always been a minute-by-minute-type of guy. I always considered predicting or thinking about the future as being too typical. I thought to myself, *How the hell did I end up here?*

My somewhat careless behavior has finally caught up to me. I never had any intentions of hurting Natalie. She was fun to hang and be intimate with, but I've never thought about her being long term. Now *Lisa*—she was most definitely the long-term type, but her career ambitions were greater than mine. Our careers didn't allow us to reap the full benefits of our union. We decided to mutually separate. Well, it was more like *she* decided to take a position in Seattle, and I refused to leave the comfort and security of my work situation here in Tennessee. I can admit I was bitter for a while, but in the midst of my bitterness, I met Natalie. I can remember it like it was yesterday. Lisa had just picked up her last bit of belongings from my two-bedroom apartment. I peered through the blinds and watched the rain tap on my windowpane.

In addition to Lisa leaving, I was irked by the loss of another black body at the hands of a systemic culture. The news was on in the background and the reporter was giving the sordid details. The number of killings at the hands of police continued to grow, and I wanted to do something about it, but didn't know what.

I turned it off and left. I had scheduled a meeting with my insurance agent, Jackson. I had some questions about my insurance policy. Jackson was also one of my best friends. When I entered the office, I noticed a new face on the premises. I gave Jackson *the* look, and he introduced me. "Natalie, I want you to meet my client and good friend Marcus Colbert." Her sun-kissed skin was smooth with no blemishes. She wasn't as attractive as Lisa, but her body was the engine that would eventually move this vehicle.

"Nice to meet you, Mr. Colbert," she replied.

"No need to be formal. Call me Marcus." When I reached out to shake her hand, her scent reached out to me. Now that Lisa was in my rearview, I needed a distraction, and what a distraction she would turn out to be.

It was now 11:35 in the evening, and I was three Jack and Cokes deep. I sat at the bar with my all-black T-shirt with bold white letters that expressed that Black Lives Matter. The crowd was steadily dispersing. I signaled for the bartender to close out my tab. As I reached for my wallet, my phone began to vibrate. A part of me was hoping it was Natalie. I mean, I really didn't want to hurt her. I know she must have thought that I had intentions of running away from our newfound responsibility, but that was not the case. I didn't fear the responsibility; I just didn't want that responsibility with her. In my mind, it was as simple as that. My phone vibrated again. As the bartender passed me the check and my credit card, I picked up the phone and noticed two new messages . . . one text and one voice mail. I began to read the text:

GREAT PRESENTATION 2DAY. WE ARE INDEED A DYNAMIC DUO. REST EASY AND WHATEVER BURDEN YOU WERE CARRYING TODAY SHALL PASS.

Kristine always knew the right things to say. The other message wasn't from Natalie, but rather my mother. I immediately remembered that I was supposed to call her to discuss my baby sister, Mia's, graduation party. "I'll call her tomorrow," I whispered to myself as I placed the phone in my back pocket. I had a nice little buzz going on. I wasn't drunk, but I was feeling good. A nightcap from Natalie would have been the next move for the night, but *now* was definitely not the time. I gathered my keys and left a nice tip for the bartender. I was hoping I was able to do what Kristine had suggested in her text . . . rest easy. However, I knew this was going to be a Sleepless in Seattle-type of night.

Chapter 3

NATALIE

I called in sick today and went to the doctor. A home pregnancy test had given me the preliminary answers I needed. Now, I wanted it confirmed by a physician. I didn't want to go to my primary care physician. She was a friend of my mother's, and I didn't need that drama. Since my mother passed away three years ago, Dr. Adina Frank had appointed herself my surrogate. I guess it was only natural since she was there the day I was born. She and my mother were best friends in college, and when my mother went into labor right after finishing her senior year, her best friend was there instead of my father. I never met my father. My mom said he just wasn't ready for a family, and when she told him she was pregnant, he suddenly wanted no part of her or me. She never even tried to find him after he left town. She said she was too busy raising me to go try to force a man to be a father. I tried, after I turned 18, and discovered he died at the age of 25 from a drug overdose. I pray to God Marcus will man up and be a father.

I chose a local clinic that catered to low-income families. That way, I could pay out of pocket and the visit wouldn't be recorded by my insurance. I wanted to keep this quiet for now. I had already peed in a cup, and now I was waiting for the results. A young lady who looked no older than 21 called my name, and I followed her to a private room. There was a bench and a chair inside. I sat on the bench and she sat on the chair.

"My name is Charlotte, and I'll be going over your test results with you. Your test did reveal that you are medically pregnant."

Medically? I thought. *What the hell does that mean?*

"Do you wanna keep it?" she said in a voice that held no emotion.

Was she serious? Was it that easy to ask a woman if she wanted to have an abortion?

I nodded my head yes. Then, I nodded no.

"I don't know," I blurted out, and then tears began to roll down my face.

She reached over to a box in the corner and handed me a couple of tissues. Neither her face nor her voice had developed any warmth. It was obvious she had done this hundreds of times.

"I understand. This isn't a decision to be taken lightly. You are very early in your pregnancy, so you still have time. However, if you decide to have the abortion, we need to run some tests to make sure you are fit for the procedure. If you don't do it today, you will need to come back. We offer two kinds of abortions here. The surgical one is the most common and least expensive. During it, we gently suction the fetus out of your uterus."

That didn't sound comfortable at all. I could just imagine them taking a vacuum tube, shoving it up my twat, and then turning it on. She continued with her emotionless talk. "The other is a medicinal, or chemical, abortion. We will give you medication that forces your body to expel the fetus. It costs more, but it is less invasive. You pop a few pills, and by the next day, you will no longer be pregnant."

I hoped this chick wasn't planning to be a doctor. Her bedside manner sucked. I decided I needed more time to think about it. I thanked her for her time and walked out into the lobby where my best friend Manny was waiting for me.

I'd had male best friends since kindergarten. I always got along with the boys better than the girls. They just understood me better. When I told Manny what happened in the bathroom with me and Marcus, he insisted that he come with me to the clinic. He felt I should have someone there to support me. I nodded to let him know that I was definitely pregnant. He hugged me and kissed me on the forehead.

"It's going to be all right, Nat. Let's get out of here. I'll take you to lunch."

I suggested we go to the Panera Bread located close by. Now that I was eating for two it was imperative that I implement more than hot fries, chicken, and soda into my diet. It was only 11 a.m., so the restaurant wasn't crowded yet, but it would be shortly. We ordered our food and waited for the buzzer the young lady who took our order gave us to vibrate, indicating that it was ready.

"I think I'm going to have an abortion," I said.

Manny gave me a puzzled look. "Okay. Why?"

I shrugged. "I don't want a baby by a man who doesn't want me."

Manny was 34 years old with two children by two different women, and he wasn't with either one of them. So I didn't expect him to be on my side.

"You know it *is* possible to have a good co-parenting situation with someone you are not married to. I'm cool with both my baby mommas, and I see my kids regularly," he said.

"I know, but when I was a little girl playing house, I was always a wife and mother. Never a baby momma, and I don't think I need to be one now."

Manny looked at me and shook his head. "First, you aren't a little girl. Nat, you are a grown woman, and if you didn't want kids, you and lover boy should have taken the necessary precautions. I would have strangled Felecia and Tara if they had even thought about killing my kids."

"Manny, can you try to see this from my side? This isn't about you. I don't know what Marcus is going to do. I could very well end up raising this baby alone. I don't *want* to be a single parent. I saw how my mother struggled to take care of me and my brother."

"You right, Nat. My fault. And since you brought up your mother, you know Ms. Sylvia wouldn't approve. As religious as she was, if she were here and you said that, she'd probably rub you down with holy oil and then force you to sit there while she read the Bible to you. I think you should take the time to really think about this, *and* you should tell Marcus what you're considering. As the father, he has a right to know."

"This isn't about what my mother would do. She's not here to help me raise or provide for this child. I am. I'm just a secretary. I'm barely making $30,000 a year. As for Marcus, I already know what he's going to say. You should have seen the look of dread on his face when the pregnancy test came out positive. He would be relieved if I ended this pregnancy. He'd probably even offer to pay for it."

"Every young man panics when he finds out he's about to be a father. Now that he's had a day to think about it, he might feel differently. I've only talked to him a couple of times, but he seemed like a stand-up guy. He may surprise you," said Manny.

"Maybe. Can we change the subject?" This was too much too soon. I had some decisions to make for myself, and as far as I was concerned, neither Marcus nor Manny had the final say.

"Sure," said Manny. "But one more thing. You seem to just be focusing on the negative aspects of having this child. Consider the positives. Children can bring a lot of joy into your life. I'm a better man because of Manuel Jr. and Rachel. I can't imagine my life without them. And you know how much they love their godmother, Nat Nat. You could have all that love they give you in your home every day from someone with your DNA." Just then, our red buzzer vibrated and lit up to indicate our food was ready. Good thing because I was starving.

Later that night, I stared at my phone. I wanted to call Marcus, but for some reason I couldn't. I knew in my heart he needed some space. He needed time to digest the news. He was probably at the bar having a few drinks to help him unwind. It must be nice to be a guy. If they don't want a kid, all they have to do is throw the mother the deuces and never look back. I have nowhere to run. Everywhere I go this little one is going to be right with me.

I went to the bathroom and wrapped my hair with a silk scarf. I got a retouch over the weekend, and I was determined to keep my hair looking like I just left the salon. While looking in the mirror, I raised up my pajama shirt and looked at my stomach. I don't know why I did that. It was way too early for me to be showing. I tried to imagine me with a big stomach. I rubbed my stomach. It would have been nice if Marcus was there to rub it. He often rubbed my abs as we lay in bed after having sex. It was Monday. Mondays were usually rough for him, and he would come over that evening to de-stress. Sometimes, we'd lay on the couch and watch a movie. Some nights I cooked. Other nights we ate out. A couple of times, I ran him a hot bath and climbed in with him. If he seemed really tense, I gave him a massage. I have some special oil that heats up when you touch it that he loves. One thing was for sure . . . No matter what we did, the night was going to end with sex unless it was my time of the month. Unbridled, passionate, carnal SEX that was what had brought us to this point.

I remember the day we met at the insurance office. I knew I wanted to get to know him better the moment we locked eyes. He looked so sexy in his Polo V-neck sweater that hugged his muscular chest and abs just enough to let you know they were there. I could tell by the way he looked at me, he liked what he saw too. As Marcus was leaving Jackson's office, he asked me for my number. I knew we weren't supposed to fraternize with fellow employees or clients. It was clearly outlined in the employee handbook, but I couldn't help myself. Marcus had waves in his head that were beckoning for me to rub them. I'd loved a man with waves since seventh grade when all the boys seemed to discover Duke Pomade and doo-rags. I wasn't surprised when Marcus called me a couple of days later and asked me to dinner. I don't remember much about dinner. I think we went to Red Lobster, but I do remember rubbing those waves later that night as Marcus used his God-given gifts to make me scream his name. I've been screaming it ever since. I normally don't have sex on the first date, but there was just something about him that told me he was one of the good ones. Somehow, I knew he wasn't going to have sex with me and never call me again.

It's hard to believe that I, Natalie Erin Tellis, could possibly be a mother . . . a baby momma, to be exact. I knew Marcus didn't want to be with me, so there was no reason for me to believe he would marry me. I knew better. The problem was, I would marry him with no hesitation. Some kind of way while he was entering my body he entered my heart. There was no way to fix that, but there was a way to fix this pregnancy. I picked my phone up off the nightstand and sent a very simple text.

I THINK I'M GOING TO TERMINATE THIS PREGNANCY. DON'T DRINK TOO MUCH. GOOD NIGHT.

Chapter 4

MARCUS

I guess there's truth to the old expression, "time flies when you're having fun," because last night was one of the longest nights of my life, and there was nothing fun about it. No sooner than I was about to lay it down for the rest of the night, I was caught off guard yet again. This time, I received a text from Natalie indicating that she had made a decision to abort her pregnancy. Excuse me—*our* pregnancy. While I fully support a woman's right to do as she pleases with her body, I also believe that a decision of this magnitude should come from both fronts. Was I an ass about the situation when she first told me? Yes. I'll admit it—that was my mistake, but how do you respond positively to something like that without leading someone on? If I would have said something to the likes of, "Wow, this is great. I'm looking forward to it," wouldn't that be sending false hopes of a future of *us* together? Over time, in the back of my mind, I knew her love for me was more than just the lust for casual sex. Her touch began to feel more than just a seductive gesture. It was something more. Something I didn't necessarily want or need.

In the morning, I decided to take a run to clear my mind. I missed the routine of getting an early-morning stride before getting my day started. I've always been a runner dating back to my track and field days in high school. I was pleased with my decision to move to

Brentwood. The suburb was located right outside of Nashville, and I loved the scenery. This was quite a change for someone who grew up like me. Don't get me wrong, I grew up in a loving home, but we weren't always financially equipped. We may have been poor in terms of money, but we were rich on the inside. That's another reason why abortions never sit well with me. I could have easily been aborted. My parents weren't married when I was conceived. My mother was fresh out of high school and my father worked in a manufacturing plant. They got married and made it work. But they had something Natalie and I don't — love. My parent were madly in love when I was conceived. I must say, they did a hell of a job raising and providing for me and my sister. I am now what most people would consider to be successful, and my sister has received a full scholarship to Fisk University.

Near the end of my jog, I was intrigued by people watching. Something in particular caught my attention. There was what I assumed to be a couple taking a morning run together. The woman was very attractive. I would estimate that she was about 5 foot 7. She had a nice frame with one of those faces you would see on the cover of a magazine. She and her runner-in-crime were moving stride for stride like symmetrical parts. I always envisioned that was what life would be like for me and Lisa, the two of us—taking the world by storm, stride for stride, side by side.

I ended up stopping at a nearby gas station to replenish my body fluids. Tennessee in the month of July was H.O.T. One would think there would be some type of relief in the morning. However, the humidity in the early mornings was just as dreadful as the midday heat. My shirt was drenched in sweat. I tried my best to soak in some of the sweat with my towel, but it was no use.

I was greeted by a police officer on his way out the door with coffee in hand. The cashier was a Caucasian woman who looked like she was in her late 30s to early 40s. Her face showed signs of life regret. I placed my bottle of water on the counter as I pulled a five dollar-bill from my pocket. *Regret.* That was a word that I never wanted to be part of my vocabulary. I was raised to live life with no regrets. You take what life dishes out and avoid situations that could be detrimental to your future. I guess you can say I haven't been doing such a good job at that lately. As the cashier handed me my change, I told her, "Have a great rest of the day." She looked at me as if she was shocked I greeted her. She replied, "Thank you. I needed that. May God bless you and your situation."

While in the shower, I was still taken aback by what the cashier had told me. *May God bless you and your situation* kept playing in my mind like a scratched CD. Life can be funny at times. You always tend to get wake-up calls in the most unlikely places. As I stood there deep in thought, the hot water helped ease my physical pain, but I needed something to heal this yearning I had for a sexual escapade. I don't know what it was about the morning time, but for some reason, that's when my sexual prowess was at its best. With Natalie not around to ease this sexual distress, I almost decided to take matters into my own hands. I decided to pass on that temptation and proceeded to step out of the shower. I turned to my right and looked at the man in the mirror, but could only see the top portion of my eyes. I opened the door to give the bathroom some ventilation. As I began to wipe some of the steam from the mirror, I overheard the news reporter discussing the situation of the young lady who had supposedly hung herself in her jail cell. Matters such as that made me rethink my career decisions. It was times like those that made me wish I had gone to law school. I could use the legal system to fight injustice at a higher level and make a difference.

Before I headed out the door for work, I reached for my watch that sat atop the manufactured fireplace mantel. Natalie had bought me the watch not too long ago for my birthday. I knew I had to respond to her sometime soon, but I needed to gather my thoughts some more before we spoke. I didn't want to engage in a conversation of this magnitude via text messages. This was something that two adults should be able to speak about face-to-face or over the phone. I looked at my watch and realized that it was only 6:30. I had another hour and a half before I had to report to work.

I decided that I would stop by the local coffee shop to grab a quick pick-me-up since I had some time to burn. The office was less than 5 miles from my home, so traffic wasn't too bad of an issue. As I pulled out my work laptop to review the daily reports, I was interrupted by a familiar face and a sweet voice.

"Hey, you. Long time no see."

I stood up and provided a light hug as I replied, "Indeed it is. How are things with you?"

"I've just been *working, working, working* day and night," she replied with her best imitation of one of my favorite Michael Jackson songs. The familiar face with the sweet voice was Chanel. She was a friend and former coworker of Lisa's. I'd always found her to be very attractive. She always reminded me of one of my favorite new actresses, Yaya DaCosta. I noticed she had cut her hair into a short fade and the hair she had left was a mass of curls. It looked good on her.

"So, how are things with you and Lisa?"

I knew that question was coming up. I knew good and well she knew that Lisa and I weren't an item or on speaking terms anymore. I took the question as either one or two things . . . she would give the rundown report back to Lisa, or she wanted to see if I was free long enough from Lisa to explore possibilities with her. You know women like to play those types of games. In your mind, you think they're asking you a simple question, but in their mind, it's a calculated method to decode an ulterior motive. Therefore, I decided to play it safe and replied, "Things are well. She's on the West Coast doing her thing. You can't knock a girl with ambition," I said somewhat sarcastically.

She stood there as if she was waiting for me to elaborate on my answer. I looked into her beautiful brown eyes with my morning appetite yet to have been fulfilled. I caught myself from gazing too hard. *Get it together, Marcus, that's why you're in the predicament that you're currently in,* I thought to myself.

"Well, it was good seeing you. Maybe I'll see you around town sometime," she said.

"Maybe," I replied. I stood up again and gave her another hug, but this time it was more firm. I wanted to feel more of her bodily embrace. "Take care, Chanel, and stay out of trouble."

She smiled and as she began to walk away she said, "Me? Trouble? How would you know?"

She abruptly stopped and turned to hand me a flyer. "If you're not too busy this evening, you should stop by." She winked as she was on her way out the door.

The flyer was an invitation to an open forum on police brutality and community protection. It was being sponsored by a local group who was affiliated with the Black Lives Matter movement. There were two reasons I was not going to miss the meeting. One was my passion and love for the people, and the other reason was walking out the door.

As I watched Chanel walk away, I slightly shook my head and smiled. When she exited the establishment, the bell rang on the door. And just like that, things were back to normal. It was as if the bell snapped me out of a trance. I was back in the real world with my real-world problems. I knew I couldn't keep having these boyhood-type fantasies as if I wasn't dealing with real manhood issues. I looked at my watch and decided it was indeed time to reach out to Natalie. I grabbed my cell phone from its case and sent the following text . . . WE NEED TO TALK. CAN I COME OVER AFTER WORK?

Chapter 5

NATALIE

I didn't sleep well last night. How could I? There were no easy answers here, and whichever one I chose, lives would be altered. I finally fell asleep around 4 a.m. but woke up at 6 a.m. I didn't have to be at work until 9 a.m. but I decided to go ahead and start my day. Busying myself would keep me from wondering why Marcus hadn't called. Maybe he doesn't care.

I took a shower and got dressed. I dressed Pepper too in a stylish doggie jacket with a matching collar. He was going to the vet today for his shots, and I wanted him to look nice. I didn't feel like cooking breakfast, but I needed to eat. I dropped off Pepper and stopped by McDonald's drive-thru and ordered a bacon, egg, and cheese biscuit, along with hash browns and a cup of coffee. Then, I drove to the park. I still had about an hour to go before I had to be at work, and I was in no mood to get there early. I rolled down the window and sat in the car, quietly eating my food while some silly morning show played on the radio. What right did they have to crack jokes and laugh like all was right with the world? Didn't they know that there were people out there with real problems?

I gazed out of my window at a squirrel scurrying through the park. He looked like he didn't have a care in the world. It must be nice to live a life where your only task in life was to dodge cars and gather acorns. Then *he* appeared, and he was gorgeous. Jogging toward me in basketball shorts with his shirt tucked in the waist was my ex-boyfriend Lionel. The last time I saw him was at my mother's funeral, and he looked better than ever. Lionel and I dated in college. He was a few years older than I. Couple that with his maturity and you had a 30-year-old going on 50. We dated for about a year, but he was just too serious for me. He wanted to get married and start a family six months after he met me. I was able to convince him to slow down a little, but on Christmas when he produced a ring, I knew I had to end things. I just couldn't give him what he wanted. I was only 20 and hadn't really lived yet. Now that I'm older, more mature, and ready for a stable long-term relationship, I regret my decision. He was definitely the one who got away. I hoped he would jog right past me without seeing me, but he noticed me right away and jogged over to my Toyota Camry and tapped on the passenger-side window for me to let him in. I really wasn't in the mood for conversation, but I didn't want to be rude.

He got in and gave me the widest grin. He looked so happy. "Fancy seeing you here. What's up, beautiful?" He gently kissed me on the cheek. I could feel some of the sweat from his top lip on my face, but I didn't care. He then began to use his shirt to wipe some of the sweat off his chest.

"Sorry about sweating in your car." I tried not to stare as beads of perspiration ran down his chiseled chest. He had milk chocolaty goodness written all over him. If I wasn't in such a crappy mood I probably would have enjoyed the view.

"It's okay. It's good to see you. I just came here to try to kill some time before I head to work."

"I heard that. How have you been?"

"I'm fine."

"You don't look okay. As a matter of fact, you look tired. What's wrong, Butterfly?"

"Don't call me that," I said.

"Why not? You'll always be my Butterfly. Even with tired eyes you're still beautiful." He smiled his 1,000-watt smile.

I ignored his comment. I was not about to engage in a trip down memory lane. "How's the wife and the kid?"

"Oh, they're wonderful. We're expecting another one in two months."

"Congratulations," I said. Next thing I knew, my eyes began to well up with tears. Why was I always crying?

"Butterfly, what's wrong?" Lionel reached out to comfort me, but I pulled away.

"Nothing," I stammered. "Look, it was nice seeing you, but I gotta go now."

"Don't go. What's wrong? Let me help you."

I wiped the tears that were streaming down my face with my hand. "Lionel, please get out of my car and let me go. I need to go now," I said.

"I know you well enough not to push, but if you need me, you can call. A part of me still loves you, you know."

He always was a sweetheart. "I know, but you can't help me. No one can. Thanks for trying, though."

Lionel reluctantly exited my car. Then, I backed out of the parking space and sped away as fast as I could. Once I was on the street, headed toward my job, I grabbed some tissue from the glove compartment. What was wrong with me? I'm not a crier, and now it seems like that's all I do. Is this what pregnancy does to you? Was I going to be an emotional wreck the entire time? I knew what I had to do. I finished wiping my face and then dialed the number for the clinic and made an appointment to get my tests completed for the abortion the next day. It was Tuesday. I could take the tests tomorrow, and if all went well, I could do it Thursday. I opted for the medicinal abortion. I didn't want someone suctioning anything out of me. Just as I pulled up to work, I got a text from Marcus asking if we could talk after work. Sure we could, but it wasn't going to do any good.

I must have looked a mess because before noon at least three people had asked if I was all right. Jackson seemed unusually concerned. I wondered if Marcus told him I was pregnant. Jackson was aware that we were seeing each other, even though it was against company policy. He never said anything to me or anyone else in the office, as far as I knew. That's probably because he had slept with a couple of the other secretaries and an adjuster from what I'd heard. I know he would have worked his way around to me eventually if Marcus hadn't gotten to me first. I caught him staring at my booty on more than one occasion. I tried to stay in my cubicle most of the day. Five o'clock couldn't come fast enough, and when it did, I picked up Pepper and then went straight home and put on our pajamas. I was tired but still couldn't sleep. We lay on the couch in our master and doggie jammies flipping through TV channels and eating snacks to pass the time. I ate potato chips, and Pepper ate doggie jerky.

Around 6 p.m. I heard a knock on the door. I figured it was Marcus, but when I opened it, there was my little brother, Jessie. Calling Jessie *little* is actually quite laughable. He's a professional bodybuilder, and everything about the man is massive. He looks like a black Incredible Hulk . . . bulges everywhere. He's been in a few competitions and usually places either first or second. I was very surprised to see him. He's been so busy training and competing the last couple of years that visits are rare.

"What are you doing here? Don't you know how to call?" I said.

"It's good to see you too, Nat. I came over because I was worried about you. Lionel called and said he saw you in the park today and you were very upset. He said you were crying, and we both know you don't cry unless something is seriously wrong. I knew if I called you, you would try to tell me it was nothing. So, I took the liberty of calling Manny, and he told me everything."

"He did what? Wait until I talk to those two." Lionel and my brother belonged to the same fraternity and became friends after Jessie joined grad chapter. Manny loves my brother like family. They were both superstar athletes in high school and somehow formed some weird jock bond. Not to mention, Manny was always at my house when we were younger. His parents were always arguing about something so he would come to our house to avoid being pulled in the middle of them.

"Come here, girl." My brother pulled me into his arms, and once again, the tears began to flow.

He held me tighter. "What's this all about, Nat? All this ain't necessary. You're going to be okay. I don't know who this dude is, but right now, he don't even matter. I ought to punch him in the face for treating my sister like some jump off. You listen to me. We ain't killing no babies. If I have to take care of my nephew, I will. The two of you will be fine. I'm doing really well with my bodybuilding. By next year, I'll be rolling in dough from prize money and endorsements. I'm even thinking about getting into acting. It worked for Arnold Schwarzenegger. Look at how well The Rock is doing! I look better than both of them combined."

I laughed. My brother was never short on confidence. "I've just been feeling so alone. Thank you, Jessie. I love you. How do you know it's a boy?"

"Just a hunch." He stepped back slightly so he could look at me but never took his huge arms from around me. I felt like a comforted dwarf. "I know I haven't been around much, but I'm still your brother. I'm as close as your phone. Everything is going to be fine. I got you, girl. Now, put away those tears. Save them for a real problem. You go to the bathroom and wash your face. Then come back in here and let's talk. And stop dressing that dog like it's human. You two look ridiculous."

My brother always had a way of making me feel better. He was three years younger than I but always behaved as if he were older, and he took his job to protect me quite seriously. Every now and then, he went a little overboard with it, but I knew he meant well. Since Momma died, we are all each other has.

I followed my brother's instructions and went to the bathroom to wash my face and blow my nose. I looked a hot mess. I had serious bags under my eyes from lack of sleep. My face was red and puffy, and my hair had somehow worked its way out of the ponytail I put it in when I got home. I fixed my face, redid the ponytail, exited the bathroom, and entered the living room. What I saw made me stop dead in my tracks. Jessie and Marcus were both in the living room, but there was one big problem. They were staring each other down as if they were about to fight. When did he get here? I didn't hear anyone at the door. Marcus worked out regularly and was in great shape, but I knew if Jessie hit him, he was in big trouble. Pepper had gotten in on the action too, but he didn't know which side to pick. He loved them both. One second his teeth were bared and he was growling at Marcus, and the next, he had turned his body in the other direction and was growling at Jessie.

"Jessie, no! What are you doing?" I screamed

"I'm protecting my family. I know this fool told you to have an abortion. Maybe I should show him what it feels like to have the life sucked out of him."

"Dude, you don't know what you're talking about. I didn't tell her to have an abortion, but if you put your hands on me, I promise we gon' be moving furniture all up in this place. I ain't never scared," said Marcus.

Marcus was usually so calm and reserved. I'd never seen him like this. It was kind of sexy. His jaw was clenched. His eyes were narrowed, and his body was in that get-ready-to-whoop-somebody stance. It was obvious he wasn't scared, but he probably should have been. In his youth, my brother had severe anger management issues and would take his anger out on anyone who was dumb enough to engage in a physical confrontation with him. It got better after my mother put him in counseling and he joined the school wrestling team, and he even did some boxing. He was one hell of a fighter. I ran over and stood in between the two of them, but I faced Jessie so I could talk some sense into him. I didn't want bloodshed in my home. Once Pepper saw whose side I was on, he bared his teeth at Jessie. Now, I not only had to worry about Jessie attacking Marcus but

Pepper attacking Jessie as well. I had to diffuse this situation quickly.

"Jessie! Stand down please. He didn't ask me to get an abortion. I made that decision all on my own."

Marcus looked at me. "What? You already made the decision. Natalie, you didn't kill my baby, did you? Please tell me you didn't kill my baby."

So he did care. Jessie relaxed. I guess that's all he needed to hear. I continued to keep my back turned toward Marcus and ignored his question for the moment.

"Jessie, do you mind leaving us alone so we can talk?"

"Yeah, I'll give you some space, but remember, I got you. Neither one of us had a daddy, and we turned out just fine."

"Thanks." I stood on my tiptoes and kissed him on the cheek. "I'll call you tomorrow."

"You do that." Then he turned his attention to Marcu. "And you, I didn't mean to flex on you, man, but this girl means the world to me. I know this ain't none of my business, but my sister is a good woman. The kind you wife, not one night. If you don't want to be with her, you shouldn't be having sex with her."

"Jessie! Go home." This was embarrassing. My brother and I had never discussed my sex life, and we weren't about to start now. Besides, the decision to engage in sex with no commitment was mutual. It wasn't like Marcus made me do it.

"I'm going, but this fool can't be treating you like this. A man takes care of his responsibilities, and a woman's heart is a fragile thing. He needs to put himself in my place. He wouldn't want nobody treating his sister or his mom like this. Give this man the answer to his question. I'm interested to see if he's gon' handle his responsibilities. I'm out, but I'm watching, fool."

"Take a good look because you'll probably be seeing more of me. I'm not hard to find. For the record, I care about your sister, but I suggest you stay out of our business," said Marcus.

Jessie gave Marcus a smirk that said, *I'll break you in half without even trying.* Then, he left.

My brother had some nerve trying to lecture anyone on women, as many women as he's run through. He's just been careful not to get anyone pregnant. I kept my body in front of Marcus until I was sure Jessie had gone. Then I let out a sigh of relief. Pepper seemed to be happy with the outcome and went back to eating his doggie jerky. That was intense. I turned around to face Marcus. His entire face had softened but wore a look of great concern. His dark brown eyes were searching me in an attempt to find an answer in my face or body language, but I gave him none. Part of me wanted to make him suffer the way I suffered all those hours when he didn't respond to my text.

"Natalie, baby, please answer my question. Did you already have the abortion?"

His eyes were begging me for an answer. I dropped my head. It's not in me to be mean. "No, but I called to make the appointment. It's scheduled for the day after tomorrow."

Chapter 6

MARCUS

I tell you, these past couple of days has been like an episode of the *Twilight Zone*. No sooner than I was about to finish my third knock on Natalie's door, I was greeted by a Kimbo Slice-looking brother. Once we read each other, he said, "You must be Marcus." I didn't know who this fool was or what Natalie had told him about me, so I immediately went into defense mode. For all I knew this could have been some payback-style setup for what she perceived to be my isolation from our newly found situation. Before the situation was about to get out of hand, Natalie had walked into the living room to diffuse it. I would be lying if I didn't say I was relieved. That Bluto-looking dude probably would have snapped me like a wishbone, and my wish was to not be in that situation. I don't think Popeye or I could have eaten enough spinach to overtake him. However, I would have gone down swinging.

I was glad to learn that it was her brother, Jessie, and not some guy she paid to cause me bodily harm. But I wasn't feeling him, and it was obvious that he wasn't feeling me. After he left, I began to calm myself. I was pleased to hear that she hadn't already proceeded with the abortion. We stood there in awkward silence. I could tell she had been crying. I wanted to reach out and hold her and profess my love for her. But the truth of the matter was, I wasn't sure I was *in* love—in *like*, but not in *love*. I must admit, though, she was looking mighty good in those pajamas. I decided to bring some comfort to our uncomfortable situation.

"How did things go at the vet?"

With a puzzled look, she asked, "How did you know Pepper had to go to the vet?"

I pointed toward the whiteboard in the kitchen. She put her entire life on that thing. "I took a wild guess."

Unwillingly, she cracked a smile and replied, "Smart-ass."

Once I saw her smile, I knew I could ease my way into the serious conversation we needed to have. I headed toward my favorite seat in the room—the chase. We shared some good times on that chase, and by the way she was looking in those pajamas, I wouldn't have minded doing some long overdue making up. Evidently, Pepper was thinking the same thing as he ran and jumped in my lap as soon as I sat down. I reached for the remote control. It seemed as if Natalie was watching one of those reality shows that I desperately despised.

"So after no word from you in almost two days, you think you can just demand control of the remote?" Natalie stated as she walked up to the television to turn it off. I didn't mind, because I didn't come over to watch television. I came to get some type of understanding.

"How have you been?" I asked.

She nonchalantly answered, "As good as I can be."

She was cold—just stone-cold. I knew I had to work a little harder to crack that exterior. However, I had to be smart about it. Again, I didn't want to come off as if I was trying to establish some type of fairy-tale relation-ship. For the longest time, I thought that her emotions and actions were a result of her brainwashed cells from watching those horrendous shows from the idiot box. But after getting to know her in a short span of time, I understood that she just wore her raw emotions on her sleeve. Pepper darted from my lap and ran to be with Natalie on the love seat. Her face seemed to be glowing, but she looked tired. I began to imagine her as the mother of my child. How would she approach child rearing? Was she going to be one of those *friend*-parents, or was she going to be a *parent*-parent? These are the questions I would eventually need answers to.

"Look. I know that I have been an ass. I know this, but you must understand my position."

She flashed a look indicating to me that my question was not the key to unlocking her uneasiness. I continued, "I want for us to do this—*together*."

"What does that mean?" she asked.

"The process. I want to be here in the now and for the duration."

"So when you say *here*—what does that exactly mean?"

My God. This was tougher than I anticipated. I didn't want to keep playing the double-meaning game. So I decided to lay out all the cards on the table. I attempted to be delicate in my approach. After all, I knew she had been emotionally fragile since we last saw each other. I didn't want to add any unwanted stress to her. It wasn't her fault that we were in this predicament. Hell, she was the one who suggested that we use protection each time we were intimate. It wasn't until recently that we were both at a comfort level with each other to begin having unprotected sex. I mean, we both were tested, so it wasn't like we were a threat to each other in terms of STDs. We also were monogamous, so that was additional assurance. I mean, I trusted her, and she trusted me, so that's how we rolled.

"I mean *us* working together as a *partnership*."

"This is not a business deal from work that you have to close, Marcus. I think we would need to be a little more than *partners* in this situation."

"Maybe my use of words is not the best. When I say partnership, I mean—being the parents for our future child."

She let out a slight exhale. I knew that wasn't the answer she was looking for, but I knew that it, at least, had put her a little at ease. She began to look toward the ceiling, and I attempted to try to read her mind. I couldn't help it; it did feel like a business transaction. The businessman in me wouldn't have it any other way. My job has always involved me reading the emotions and body language of my clients. This situation was no different. I knew what "hot buttons" to push, and I was ready for any rebuttals she would throw my way. I laid out my proposal. Now I was just waiting on her to sign her name on the dotted line to close the deal. I've been a closer all my life, and I didn't plan on it being any other way.

I continued to sit quietly. Sometimes awkward silence was a good thing in my world of business. She exhaled again before turning toward me. She seemed relaxed and less tense. She uncrossed her arms and grabbed the nearest throw pillow. Clutching the pillow to her chest she asked me, "Can I trust you?"

Trust was a strong word. It was a word that I didn't take for granted. Trust is what makes or breaks relationships. I trusted Lisa when she said that nothing would get in the way of our relationship. The family of Trayvon

Martin trusted that the system would provide some justice. As kids, we all *trusted* that our parents would forever protect and provide for us. I bet Natalie's mom trusted her father when he said he would always be there. And most importantly, I trusted that God would lead me. So as you can see, the word *trust* is fragile.

I replied, "Yes. You can trust me."

She bit down on her bottom lip and started rocking slightly back and forth still clutching the pillow. Pepper was doing a little dance on the carpet. You know, that whole chasing-your-tail deal. She said one simple word that indicated that she was ready to close the deal.

"Okay."

When I got back to my car, I sat there for a second. I knew the road would be tough, but I had convinced myself that I was ready to move forward. In my mind, I was already a father. I could use a little extra motivation to slow down my life a little. I needed something—I mean, *someone*, to love unconditionally. I needed that because my life outside of work was a total wreck. I could no longer mask my happiness behind a desk. I needed someone to come home to that didn't care if I was closing deals. I guess I needed someone to unconditionally love me too. I looked in my rearview mirror that was positioned toward Natalie's living room window. I saw the light go off and was replaced by the light from the television. I envisioned her all snuggled up on the couch with Pepper mirroring her every move. I slowly began to back up and make my way back to a place that was empty—home.

On my way home, I decided to call my mother back from the other day. I knew she would have a slight attitude since I hadn't responded in a timely manner.

You know mothers like to be the top priority, no matter what the situation was. I also called her to discuss my current predicament. I seldom discussed my relationship matters with either of my parents. Lisa and my mom had a great relationship, but it wasn't like they were phone buddies. After all, when would Lisa ever have time to do anything outside of work?

"Good evening, Mommy dearest."

"Well, it's nice to hear your voice."

I chuckled as I replied, "Sorry, Ma. I've just been a little busy at the job."

"Well, it's good to know that something is important on your list of priorities."

"Come on, Ma—that's not fair. You know there is no competition when it comes to you and your place in my heart." I knew that would add a little icing on the cake. I always sweetened up the deal with my mom. We continued to discuss the usual. I listened to her complain about my dad. I listened to her provide in-depth details on her journey at the grocery store. I also listened to her moan and groan about Mr. Willie and his untamed yard. She always swore that he was the cause of all her close neighbors moving or losing their homes. Gentrification never crossed her mind. However, I didn't mind listening to her angelic voice. It was the same voice that put me to sleep and at ease. It was the same voice that soothed me when I was sick. It was the same voice that disciplined me when I was cutting up. It was the same voice that taught me how to love. It was a voice that I hoped would be mimicked by Natalie to our unborn child.

I decided to steer the conversation in another direction. "So, what are your plans for Mia and her graduation?"

"Child, I guess we just gonna have it at the house. I ain't got no extra money to be renting out no damn clubhouse or whatever silliness she wants."

I laughed. "Ma, nobody does clubhouses anymore. How about I ask around town? I'm sure I can get something reasonable. I'll pay for it if that's the main concern. After all, it's not every day that your baby sister graduates from high school. That's a milestone one should never forget."

I eased my way into what I really wanted to discuss with my mother. "Hey, you remember Natalie?"

She paused for a second before responding. "The girl you been lollygagging with?"

I laughed again. I swear my mom was a trip. "Come on, Ma. We got to get your lingo game up. To answer your question, yes. She is the young lady I've been lollygagging with."

"I knew it wasn't gonna last long. She is no Lisa."

I got a little defensive about her response. One—I felt a certain way about her having little faith in my relationships. Two—she brought up the ex, which is the ultimate no-no.

"Who said we weren't together anymore?"

"Well, I only met her once, and that was by mistake. If I hadn't popped up at your place, I probably wouldn't have known she ever existed. You know you're not serious about that girl."

My mom was right. I wasn't serious about Natalie. However, that would have to change. I prepared myself as I was about to drop the bombshell on her. I was about to tell her that she was about to be a first-time grand-mother. At the tender age of 51, she was about to be the one to say yes to everything for a change. After all, her job would be to spoil the child. She no longer had to rear; that would be all on me—*and* Natalie.

"Well, she is expecting."

"Expecting what?"

"Your grandbaby . . ."

"Oh, hell nawl—MARCUS!!!"

Chapter 7

NATALIE

I felt a little more at ease after Marcus left but not much. It wasn't what he said. It was what he didn't say. He told me that I could trust him, and he would be there, but he never said he wanted this baby. I find it odd how a man with the gift of gab good enough to close multi-million dollar deals could become at a loss for words when it came to talking about his feelings. I didn't want him to go. It had been an emotional day, and I was feeling the drain from it. However, I understood his distance. I didn't like it, but I understood it. In the morning, I was going to call the clinic and cancel my appointment. I was going to have his baby. There were worst things in the world I could do. Marcus was a lot of things: sexy, driven, handsome, and honest. As far as I knew, he never lied to me about where he stood on any topic. I had no one to blame but myself for my current predicament. I engaged in a sexual relationship I knew had no future because I was lonely and horny. I took out my journal and wrote one simple sentence.

How do you stop yourself from falling in love with a man you know doesn't love you?

I turned off my television and tried to get comfortable. I needed to get some sleep, but I wished that Marcus was cuddled up with me instead of Pepper. Then it was as if I received some sudden newsflash across the tickertape in my brain. Why was I sleeping alone? It made no sense. I got up, put on some clothes, packed a bag, and left the house. I may not be able to have his heart, but I could still get him to make me feel loved.

Marcus lived in a very nice, newly erected condo in Brentwood. It allowed him quick access to his downtown office without actually having to live downtown. I knew it well. It was much nicer than my one-bedroom apartment in Antioch, but that was to be expected. He probably made three times more than I did. It didn't take me long to drive to his place. As I pulled in front, I noticed that his downstairs lights were on. I was happy to see that he was still up. This wasn't the first time I had gone to Marcus's house unannounced, but this was the first time I was going as the mother of his child. I knew he liked when I occasionally took control. He also enjoyed my little surprises. I probably should have put on some sexy lingerie, a trench coat, and heels, but I didn't want to waste time getting there. If things went my way, I wouldn't be wearing this T-shirt and jeans long. I didn't like this feeling of awkwardness between us. That just wasn't us, and it was time to put an end to it. We were always easy. One day at a time, no expectations, and that's the way I wanted it now. I missed my Marcus. I needed my lover and my friend. I rang the doorbell and waited. He opened the door wearing nothing but a pair of jogging pants. I loved his chest. He always kept it shaved and the smoothness of his skin reminded me of chocolate mousse. I probably would have stopped right there at the door and taken one of his enticing nipples in my mouth but I noticed when he smiled, he looked a little distraught.

Before he could say anything I said, "I really don't want to be alone tonight. Can I stay with you?"

He said, "C'mon in. I'm glad you're here. I just told my mom about the baby. I could use the company."

Marcus pulled me close and covered his mouth with mine. It felt good. He had the most amazing kisses.

"I missed you, Natalie. Forgive me for being an ass."

I felt a familiar friend grow hard against my leg.

"I forgive you. I missed you too," I said. I took his luscious lips in mine. Our tongues probed each other's mouths hungrily. We both knew we were about to devour the other.

I was curious to know what his mother said. I didn't know her well. We only met once. She was cordial, but it was obvious she had no idea who I was and wanted to know why I was there. I assumed that her words had upset him in some way. I took my right hand and began to gently caress his left nipple. He needed comfort, and I was more than willing to give it. The conversation about what she said would have to wait until another time. I wasn't going to kill this vibe we had going on. We didn't go about this right, but the fact of the matter was we were accustomed to each other. We had been sleeping together for months. It was a routine . . . eat, sleep, work, and amazing sex with Marcus at least 2–4 times a week depending on his work schedule. We both had what sometimes seemed like an insatiable sexual appetite. If only we were as compatible in other areas. I didn't see why we had to break our routine. It's not like I could get pregnant again.

As we began ripping each other's clothes off, I said those three forbidden words, "I love you." I don't know why I said them. They just slipped out. Marcus immediately froze. I had to quickly recover the moment. I smiled and said, "Don't say anything, just feel," and began kissing him on his neck. I knew that was a sensitive spot for him. He slowly relaxed and let out a soft moan. Mission accomplished! Then, he took his hand, guided my face upward, and kissed me again. This time more deeply, and the next thing I knew, my feet were leaving the floor, and I was being carried to his room. Marcus made love to me that night. There was no doubt about it. The passion between us was so intense. I don't know what his mother said, but I needed her to say it more often. It felt like he wanted to show me that he truly cared for me and he wasn't going anywhere. I could feel it in the very depths of my soul.

We were upright on the mattress with my legs wrapped around his waist. Face to face, breast to chest and clinging to each other tightly. As my body combined with his, I wished that love was transferrable. I would have shifted some of what I felt to him and used it like a steel chain to form an unbreakable bond for the rest of our lives. I could tell that he was almost to the point of ecstasy, but he was trying to hold back to make sure that I was satisfied. He was such a pleaser in the bedroom. Tears ran down my face, and screams escaped from my lips as I shook from his efforts. He then grasped my body tighter, and sucked hard on my earlobe while releasing a deep, throaty groan. I felt a second inner-earthquake as his warmth erupted inside me. It was magical. Marcus made me feel like no other, and I never wanted to be without him. I vowed to myself that night that I would learn what it would take to make this man love me. I didn't want to just be his baby momma. I wanted to be the number one woman in his life. I wanted my child to have a two-parent home.

I took my hands and rubbed the top of his head and whispered, "Marcus."

"Yes, baby?" he responded slightly out of breath.

"That was amazing."

He laughed and said, "Thank you but I think you had something to do with it."

"Do it again," I said seductively and then sniffed. I felt the cold wet tears that fell from my eyes slowing making their way down my face and neck.

"Are you sure you can handle it?"

"Boy, stop asking questions you already know the answer to."

"Yes, ma'am," he said and proceeded to ravage my body again until we were both too exhausted to continue. As we drifted off to la-la land, I sought to find the answers that I needed. I learned years ago if you ask a man questions when he is happy and sleepy he's less likely to lie to you. His brain is too high and too exhausted to concoct elaborate lies quickly.

"Marcus?"

"Huh?" he said in a low voice. I could tell he was almost asleep.

"Do you want this baby?"

"What? You wanna ask questions now?"

"I need to know now. Do you want this baby?"

Marcus opened his drowsy eyes and looked at me. "It's not that I *don't* want this baby, but I wish that circumstances were different. Natalie, I've kept it 100 about what I wanted from you and what I could give in return, and a baby was never part of the conversation. But it happened. He or she is coming, and I'm going to do my damnedest to be there for you during the pregnancy and be a good father."

"OK. Last question. Do I make you happy?"

"I guess so. I know you make me feel good. Tonight was one for the record books."

"You make me happy," I said.

"I'm glad." He gave me a quick peck on the lips. "Baby, get some sleep." Then he sucked gently on my bottom lip.

I loved when he did that. That was all I needed to hear for now. I nestled my naked body beneath his and lay my sleepy head in the crook of his arm. He then draped his other arm over me, and we both fell into a deep slumber.

The next morning I woke up alone, but there was a note taped to the lamp by the bed.

I had to get to work early, and I didn't want to disturb you. Breakfast is on the stove. Talk to you soon.

He was always so thoughtful. I knew nobody at work was going to be asking me what was wrong today. I was on cloud nine. I had to put together a plan that would allow me to keep feeling this way, and I knew just the person to ask to help me do it. I picked up the phone and called my godmother.

"Hey."

"Girl, you were on my list to call. Things have been so busy at the practice. How are you?"

"I'm good. I'm pregnant."

"Really? Is that a good thing?"

"I think so. I know you're busy so I'll get straight to the point. I'm in love with my child's father, but he doesn't love me. Is there a way to fix that?"

She laughed. "People kill me doing things backward. Y'all wanna have sex with a man and then ask for a relationship. Get pregnant and then get married. There is no magic potion for making a man love you. Either he does or he doesn't, but what you can do is make him need you."

"What do you mean?"

"Every man reaches a point when he's tired of the game and wants to settle down. For many of them, the decision of who to wed is more intellectual than emotional or physical. He recognizes that she brings something to his life that will help him be a better person and further his life ambitions. Kind of like the man who marries the trophy wife simply because she looks good on his arm and will help turn heads in his direction. It's like a business deal," she said.

"Funny you said that. I just told Marcus that us raising this baby wasn't a business transaction, but maybe it is."

"You can use this baby to your advantage, but you can't be obvious about it. As long as it's still in the womb his attention will be on you. Show him that you can add value to his life and that he needs you."

Natalie paused. "But isn't that like trapping a man? Shouldn't he love me?"

"Chile, love ain't got nothing to do with it. Love doesn't pay bills. It doesn't put food in your belly or win wars. It may start them, but it doesn't win them. Find out what he's lacking and then provide it. Provide it so well that he realizes he can't get it anywhere else. My next appointment is here. Congrats on the baby. You are going to make a wonderful mother. I just hate your mother isn't here to share this moment with you."

"Me too. I love you."

"I love you more."

I wasn't quite sure I agreed with her. I didn't want to trick Marcus into being with me. I wanted him to *want* to be with me. That way, I know it's going to last. You can't beat the real thing . . . right?

Chapter 8

MARCUS

It's been nearly four months since Natalie and I decided to come to terms with this pregnancy. I'm happy to say that we're still in a good place. I no longer feel the pressure of being obligated to having a relationship outside of the preparation of being co-parents. I'll admit, it was rocky for a minute. Her mood swings were beginning to be a challenge. For the past couple of weeks that has subsided. We haven't been playing house as of late. The changes that are happening with her body have been playing with her mental space. She was beginning to feel as if I no longer found her attractive. That wasn't the case at all. My recent distance didn't have anything to do with her physical state. Things were *real* now. It's not that they haven't been—it's just that she's starting to physically show the results of our loveless affair. At least from my viewpoint, that's how it's been. But like Tina says, *What's love got to do with it?* She and I both knew that it was the sex that was holding us together. I thought about trying to make it work as far as establishing a relationship, but you can't fit a circle in a square peg. For example, I've witnessed many scenarios where the parents decided to stay together because of the child. Probably 90 percent of those scenarios ended up in divorce. In most cases, that does more damage to the child than them just being honest with themselves up front. Natalie kept hinting at it for a while, and I just had to be honest with her. She wasn't happy, but she's dealing with it. The other option and probably the route we should have taken was to not have unprotected sex. Not only were we jeopardizing our health, we were playing with lives as well.

The holiday season was right around the corner, and Jackson was hosting his company's annual holiday dinner in the next few weeks. He was unsure of what venue he wanted to utilize, so we've been patronizing a handful of new ones over the last couple of days. One of the newbies was nestled in the heart of downtown. It was an upscale restaurant with a small dance floor. The atmosphere had a nice vibe for the professionally inclined. It was becoming a premiere after-hours spot. I had heard about the place from one of my clients.

We were at the bar, and Jackson had just ordered us another round of shots. There was a group of ladies celebrating what seemed to be the engagement of one of their friends. The heavyset sister, who was celebrating the most, kept inadvertently bumping up against Jackson. On a couple of occasions she nearly knocked his drink out his hand. Bracing himself on his stool, he began to ask me about the situation with Natalie. When Jackson first heard of the pregnancy, things were a little weird. He advised that I had put him in an awkward situation. The last thing he said he wanted was some baby mama drama inside the workplace. Being that we were good friends, this pregnancy was personal for him as well. Natalie and I assured him that our situation wouldn't affect business at Smith & Noble Insurance Agency. Jackson Smith was in a great position to take over the agency once his father decided to retire. It's been in the family for two generations, and Jackson would be the third. Originally called Smith & Associates, they completed a recent merger with another prominent agency in the area, and Jackson was poised to take the independent agency to the next level. Therefore, he wanted me and Natalie to be on our best behavior.

"Did Natalie tell you she's been thinking about getting her producer's license?"

With a look of interest I replied, "No. I can't say that she has mentioned that to me." I was pleased to hear that Natalie was looking to better her situation at the agency. I always knew that it was only a matter of time before she would want to earn a little more. It would also allow her to be a little more flexible in terms of her scheduling. "Do you think she would be a good producer?"

Jackson gently shook his drink and took a sip as he replied, "You know—she's a people person. I think she can find a niche. What? You don't think she has what it takes?"

Just as I was about to answer his question, I saw a familiar face emerge within the group of celebrating ladies. Jackson noticed my attention had been placed elsewhere, and he followed my eyes. There she was, looking beautifully stunning. Her dress was screaming for me to gently remove it from her heavenly body. Even though I knew she was somewhat off-limits, that didn't stop me from envisioning what it would be like to dance to the tunes of her love box. All of a sudden, we locked eyes. Before I knew it, she was headed in my direction. Jackson glanced at me and gave me the "thumbs-up" look.

"So we meet again."

Chanel's voice was like a breath of fresh air. In my attempt to stand from my stool, I accidently bumped into the sports-talking guy sitting to my right. He shot me an irritated look. I apologized for the disturbance and proceeded with my intentions. Besides, I didn't have time to potentially get into an unnecessary altercation with another brother because of a slight nudge. Now standing on my feet, I extended my arms for an embrace. Her perfume was like the pheromones produced by the supervillain Poison Ivy. I knew I had a working brain and tongue, but for some reason, the words weren't flowing from my mouth. Finally I replied, "It's good to see you again, Ms. Chanel." I stood back, my hands still placed upon her hips. My eyes were extended toward her ring finger. I just wanted to be sure that she wasn't the one celebrating.

"I haven't been in trouble lately," she said with seduction written all over her face.

I flashed a perplexed look on my face as I replied, "What do you mean?"

"Last time we met you told me to stay out of trouble, Mr. Colbert."

We both smiled simultaneously.

"I apologize that we didn't get a chance to speak after the Black Lives Matter meeting."

She smiled as she replied, "No worries. Did you enjoy yourself?"

"Yes. It was great. You delivered a powerful speech. I left there motivated to do more."

"I'm glad, my brother."

"My apologies—how can I be so rude? Chanel, I want you to meet my friend Jackson. He's the future principal of Smith & Noble Insurance Agency." They both exchanged handshakes as they greeted each other. I continued, "Listen, if it's okay with you—do you want to find a quiet place and play a little catch-up?"

Damn. That's all I could say to myself as I was looking at this beautiful specimen of a woman that God created. I mean, Lisa was attractive. On a scale from 1 to 10, Lisa was probably a 10, but *Chanel*—she was that *plus* one as it relates to her mental space . . . which made her an 11.

"That would be fine. Let me tell my friend-girl and I'll be right back," she said.

As I watched her maneuver her way through the crowd, I immediately turned to Jackson when she was out of my view. I nudged him on the shoulder as I said, "That's the one I told you about a couple months back."

"I see ya, brother. One question, though—what about Natalie?"

Natalie? Damn! I whispered to myself. "Listen—as I've told you before—we're good with our arrangement. We're not a couple per se. We're more like partners."

"Partners, huh? Well, I just hope you know what you're doing. And most importantly—make sure it doesn't spill over to the professional realm."

I knew where Jackson was coming from. It was not my intentions to be disrespectful to him, or Natalie, for that matter. There was just some type of magnetic energy between myself and Chanel. True enough, it could have been pure lust, but as the imperfect human beings that we are, I just had to find out. I fully understood what I was potentially getting myself into, but I was almost certain that I could handle Natalie and Chanel. I would just be upfront about everything. The way I saw it was that as long as I was honest and not leading anyone on—all should be well.

***

My relationship with Natalie has been going through some more changes as of late. We no longer laughed together or had that *look* toward each other. After the conversation I had with Chanel at the bar, I decided to leave it there. It just didn't sit right in my spirit. I was wrong, and I was able to look myself in the mirror and come to grips with it. However, the thought of coming home to Natalie and dealing with the petty arguments and watching my ambitions and aspirations go down the drain was not an option for me. As a result, I began to reach out to Chanel.

For the past three weeks we've been out on four different occasions . . . you know . . . just getting to know each other beyond what we already knew. It hasn't been anything too extreme, just the basics—movies, dinner, and a nice comedy show. The vibe between us was real. I felt refreshed. I felt reenergized. I felt comfortable. She added that extra *something* that I wanted and needed in my life. But, I also felt wrong. I felt wrong because, I hadn't shared with her another major detail of my life—Natalie. I decided to let it all out.

"Wow, Marcus. That's a lot to take in this early," Chanel said after I told her about my situation.

"I understand, and I know I probably should have been up front with you earlier, but I didn't think we would go beyond just a friendship. Chanel, I have to be honest with you. I've fallen for you, and I think you feel the same way."

She didn't respond immediately. I'll admit, I was as nervous as the first time I ever called a girl on the telephone. I could no longer take the awkward silence.

"Listen. I know that's a lot to take in, but I didn't know how to tell you without seeming like a deadbeat."

She looked into my eyes. She was searching for something. It seemed as if she needed some assurance, and my eyes were the windows to my soul. Even though we'd only been kicking it for a short period of time, I knew she had raw feelings for me, and the same could be said for me.

"Do you love her?"

I sighed a little before replying. "Love? No. *But* I do care for her." I reached for her hand and continued. "The feelings I have for her are not the same as what I have for you. I know we've only been going out for a little less than a month, but I can tell you that I haven't had this much fun and felt this free since . . ."

She sensed my hesitation and completed my sentence. ". . . since Lisa?"

I set myself up for that one, but again, honesty was my best policy, so I gave her the straight-up truth. "Lisa is no longer a concern of mine. That's the past. I'm ready to move forward to a future."

"And what future is that?" she asked.

"I'm not sure, but I would like for it to involve you." *Damn.* I really do have feelings for Chanel. I felt it right in my soul. I will admit, I've never experienced this feeling with Natalie. Chanel and I haven't even been intimate yet. No kiss—no nothing.

"I like you, Marcus. I really do. You're everything I envisioned, but I need to sleep on this one. Can you give me some time?"

"Listen, take all the time you need. Trust me, I understand."

She reached for her keys and leaned for her purse. Then she paused. I thought she was about to make her decision. In the back of my mind, I was expecting her to tell me that it was over. All of a sudden, she placed her keys back on the end table. She searched through her purse and pulled out her phone. I saw the screen fade out, indicating that she had shut down her phone. She looked at me searching me again. She then replied, "Can I sleep on it *here,* with you?"

I can't explain the feeling that was jolting through my body. Here I was, sitting next to this drop-dead gorgeous woman who hit me with a proposal to stay the night. I wanted to say, *Hell yeah! You can stay,* but I kept it cool as usual. *This is the one,* I said to myself. I smiled at her as I placed my arm around her neck to pull her closer. "Yes. I would love that."

I looked at the clock on the wall and noticed that it was a little after 10. It was Sunday, so I wanted to catch up with the sports world on my favorite channel. I reached for the remote as she lay in my arms. Life was good in the Colbert residence. I felt clean. I didn't have any skeletons in the closet. I laid it all out on the table. Then I began to think, *How in the hell am I going to break this gently to Natalie?* I kissed Chanel lightly on her forehead and immersed myself into my Sunday night pleasantry. Now that I was honest with Chanel, I had to tell Natalie as well, but something deep inside my bones was telling me that it wasn't going to go as smooth as it did tonight.

Chapter 9

NATALIE

I'm sitting in the OBGYN's office for my next appointment. I haven't been feeling well. Nobody ever told me that pregnancy makes you crazy and self-loathing. I don't like the things that are happening to me or my body. I've always been able to maintain a curvaceous physique, whether I worked out or not, but as of late, I've been gaining weight at a rapid speed. The only curves I see are disproportioned. My butt is too big, my breasts are taking on this weird enlarged shape. They hurt all the time, and, of course, my stomach is protruding. I'm itching like crazy, and I'm tired of throwing up every morning. It's gross. I'm also tired all the time, which isn't helping me at work. All I want to do is sleep. Last week, I fell asleep in the ladies' bathroom while sitting on the toilet. When I got back to my desk, I had five messages from Jackson. He had been calling me because he needed me to get the call-in number for an important conference call. He missed the call. Needless to say, he was not happy.

Marcus hasn't touched me in weeks. I don't blame him, and honestly, I'm not upset about it. I don't feel attractive or sexy. He told me I still look good, but I don't believe him. I miss Marcus. He hasn't been around a lot lately. He said he has a lot to do at work. I don't really believe that either, but I guess I can blame the mood swings for that. My emotions seem to go from negative zero to 100 in an instant. One minute I'm sad, and 30 seconds later, I'm mad at the world. Two days ago, I asked him to bring me some ice cream and when he showed up, I started crying because it wasn't low fat and then yelled at him for being so inconsiderate. He left without even saying good-bye. It would be nice if I could have him beside me at night rubbing my shoulders, my stomach, and my feet. Pepper is good for a lot of things, but he can't do that.

I've been filling my time studying to get my producer's license. I figured the more money I make, the better. It's not like I have a husband to support me or something. I tried to talk to Marcus about us trying to be a couple for the sake of the baby, and he basically said he wasn't interested. I don't get it. Why was I good enough to sleep with on a regular basis, but I'm not good enough to be his girlfriend? The last couple of times he was so passionate. I just knew he felt something for me. I thought this baby would bring us closer together, but it seems to be pushing us apart. Hopefully, things will be better after today. He will be attending his first doctor's appointment with me. He couldn't make the last one because of some major deal he was working on, but I understood. I knew there would be others. Where is Marcus, anyway? They'll be calling me to the back shortly. We hadn't talked since the day before so I decided to give him a call to make sure he hadn't forgotten. The phone rang three times and a woman answered.

"Hello. I'm sorry, I must have the wrong number," I said.

"No, Natalie. You have the right number. This is Chanel, Marcus's girlfriend. He left his phone at my house this morning. I know you have an appointment today, so when I saw your number I answered, in case it was important."

"Chanel? That was thoughtful of you," I said sarcastically. "I'm at the appointment now, and Marcus hasn't arrived yet, so I was checking to see if he was still coming."

"He's on his way. He should be there shortly. I know Marcus is looking forward to it. He's really getting excited about being a father. Congratulations to both of you."

I must say she had a soothing voice, like the ones you hear on relaxation technique CDs. "Thanks. Chanel, you know who I am, but I must say that I've never heard of you. How long have you and Marcus been together?"

There was a long pause. She wasn't getting off that easy. "Don't go silent now. You were the one who decided to answer his phone."

The soothing quality of her voice left, and it was replaced by nervousness. "I was under the impression you knew. I'm sorry. This is very awkward, and I think this is a conversation you should have with Marcus."

I knew she would punk out. That was wise of her. In my condition, I was not to be played with. "Oh, no worries, Ms. Chanel, unknown girlfriend of my Marcus, I will. Have a nice day." The nerve of that man! When I need him the most, he goes and gets a girlfriend. No wonder he's been keeping his distance. He's not touching me because he's been touching someone else.

The nurse called my name. I walked toward her so she could escort me to the back but stopped at the front desk for a moment and addressed the young lady who checked me in earlier. "My child's father, Marcus Colbert, is coming. When he arrives, please tell him he can have a seat out here in the waiting room and wait for me to finish my visit, if he likes. May I have a sheet of paper?" I asked. She reached over and took a sheet of white paper out of a small printer on the side of her desk and handed it to me. I scrawled something down, folded it, and handed it to her. "Please give him this note for me."

Chapter 10

MARCUS

Who the hell is Chanel? you told me you didn't want a girlfriend. Don't even think about coming into my exam room. I HATE YOU!

Those words were all that were written on the note Natalie left me at the front desk with the clerk. She knew I was looking forward to this visit. I wanted to hear my baby's heartbeat and see him or her on the ultrasound screen. What was happening with her? I'd never known her to be mean or vindictive. Her sweet and easygoing demeanor were two of the things that attracted me to her. How did she find out about Chanel? However she found out, I didn't want it to be this way. I was trying to wait for the perfect time as I knew how vulnerable she had been as of late. I wish life was as simple as hitting the "reset" button to alter the decisions you've made. But, just like my mother always told me, "You make the bed, you lie in," and that was just what I was going to do.

I leaned on the front desk and tried my best to reason with the young lady. The way she was looking at me was as if she had read the letter; now she was sitting here judging me. Listen, I don't care how people perceive me, but I do care if their assumption is based off inaccurate or half-truths. Maybe I could reason with her.

"Listen—we've been going through a rough patch lately. Is there any way I can get in the room?"

While multitasking, she didn't even look up at me to respond. "I already told you. I can't. I was given specific instructions to hand you the note and advise you to wait until Ms. Tellis was done."

"Haven't you ever said some things you really didn't mean?"

She sighed as she put down her ink pen for a second. Both of her arms were now resting over the charts, papers, and invoices that sat atop her desk. She hesitated as she tried to get the last bit of freshness from the mint she had been sucking on. "Look, you seem like a decent man—a smart man at that. You being here says a lot in my opinion, but there are some crazies in the world. If I let you through those doors and something was to happen, then my job would be in jeopardy. Whatever y'all got going on is between y'all. It's nothing personal, but I can't let you walk through that door."

I knew when I had been defeated. She was right. There was no need for me to drag her into our personal business. I backed off and told her that I understood her position. I went back and took a seat. Several thoughts were racing through my mind. *Hell, she don't want you here . . . Why stay? How the hell did she find out about Chanel? I wonder if we'll know if it's a boy or girl. Damn, I still can't believe that in less than four months, I'm going to be a father.* While deep in thought, I watched as this young couple entered and was now at the front desk. They couldn't have been any older than Natalie and I. They were holding hands and smiling—the whole nine. I knew that was what Natalie expected of me. We had a conversation a couple weeks back discussing our little arrangement. She asked in her own way, what we would need to do to become that loving couple. We went back and forth over the issue, and then I finally told her that love is something you can't force; it has to be natural. It was at that point that I knew intimacy was out of the question, especially with my situation with Chanel. We both were being selfish in some aspects. She then proceeded to tell me that we should at least try for the baby. Honestly, that had crossed my mind. But, as I've stated before, I don't want to do it just for the baby. I don't think that would be a healthy relationship. I didn't want to raise a child in a broken home. In my mind, as long as the child had two loving parents who were involved in his or her life, then that's all that would matter.

I had to come up with a way to fix this. I then began to think about the conversation my mother and I had. When we discussed my situation she wasn't too pleased. For one, I wasn't married, and two—we weren't even a couple. With her knowing the type of person she raised, she knew I wasn't going to back away from my responsibilities. She did reiterate that the decision Natalie and I made was a lifetime decision. I initially told my mom that we knew that and we were good with our relationship. However, that was before Chanel entered the picture. I was in no rush to introduce Chanel to my parents. I didn't feel like going through the whole interrogation and explanation phase.

I waited another forty-five minutes before I walked back up to the front desk. I had to be back at work before noon, but I didn't want to go without at least having a word with Natalie. As soon as I was about to question how much longer it would take, I saw the door to my left open slowly. Natalie walked out gingerly holding her stomach. I hadn't seen her since our little ice cream mishap. Her stomach looked as if it was protruding more. I briskly walked toward the door and extended it wide enough for her to walk through. I reached for her hand, but she rejected my offer. I sensed she was a little agitated with every move that I made. Walking past me as if I was a stranger, she walked up to the front desk to receive her next appointment schedule. I walked over as well to put the date into my calendar, but I remembered that I left my phone at Chanel's place.

I asked the young lady, "Can I please have one of those reminder notes for the next appointment?"

Natalie rolled her eyes and nodded to the clerk to let her know it was okay.

I thanked the young lady as we made our way toward the front door.

"Do you want to grab a bite to eat? Are you going back to work?"

She didn't answer me. She was moving as fast as her pregnant body would allow her to. I followed behind. "NATALIE!" I called out.

She stopped in front of her car and placed her purse on top of the hood. It was a little warmer than usual for November, but there was still a cool breeze. I took off my cardigan and draped it over her shoulders. She nudged away, rejecting my offer.

"Why are you here, Marcus?"

I was taken aback by her question. "What do you mean . . . why am I here?" I extended my arm toward her belly as I continued, "I'm here because of our child."

Her eyes began to well up. "What about me?"

I leaned on the front grill of her car as I replied, "You will always be a part of my life. That's never going to change."

With tears in her eyes, she folded her arms and sniffed. "That's not what I asked you, Marcus." She shook her head as she looked away. She then spotted the same couple I had been looking at when I was sitting in the waiting room and stopped to watch them. They looked so happy. He was opening her car door. They were laughing. They seemed to be the true definition of a loving couple experiencing something beautiful— together. As they drove off, it seemed as if a switch had flicked on and Natalie was back with her mood swings.

"How the hell you gonna be there for me when you've moved on with someone else? How the hell did you even find the time to begin a new relationship? Who does that, Marcus?"

I let out a heavy sigh. I understood her position. If we were living in a perfect world, I would have loved to be with Natalie exclusively. But I don't like to live my life with hypotheticals.

"Natalie, we've discussed this numerous times. I thought you were okay with where we stand."

Her tone reached a higher level. "Well, Marcus, I lied. I'm *not* okay with it. I certainly wasn't expecting you to move on while I was *still* pregnant." A couple of tears began to roll down her cheek. "I just—I just figured we would find a way." She snatched her purse from the roof of her car and headed toward the driver's side door.

"I'm sorry, Natalie. I should have been upfront with you about Chanel."

She opened the door and got in. As she sat in the car she replied, "You're right. You *are* sorry. And you'll be *very* sorry soon enough." She slammed the door and immediately hit her locks.

I watched as she sped off from the parking lot. I just stood there, then I noticed some nosey women were dropping in on our conversation. One of them had the nerve to shake her head and scream out, "WORTHLESS." I ignored it. I knew she was probably one of those women who fed off of negativity. I began to walk back to my car as I thought about her last statement. *You will be sorry.* Something deep inside was telling me that I was about to enter a world unknown to me and I was not prepared.

Chapter 11

NATALIE

"Happy birthday, Jackson!" I came into his office bearing gifts. Today was his 40th birthday, and I had organized an entire day of surprises for him. He wasn't exactly pleased with my performance at work lately, so I had to do something to make amends. I had been working for him for almost 9 months, and he was a pretty good boss. Yet, I knew my distraction and frequent mistakes weren't going unnoticed, and they were getting on his nerves. The first gift was a card, balloons, and a massage therapist. She was in one of our empty offices setting up.

When Jackson looked up and saw me he was grinning from ear to ear like a Cheshire cat. "You remembered," he said.

"Of course, I did. I couldn't forget the birthday of the best boss in the world," I said in an animated voice.

He looked like a kid at Christmas. "You better be glad that I like surprises. What did you get me?"

"Well, the usual: a card, balloons, and we are having cake and ice cream in the breakroom in your honor later. But right now, you have a lovely massage waiting for you in Kyle's old office."

"Are you serious? I really could use one. That's very thoughtful of you, Natalie."

"It's the least I could do. I have some other surprises planned for you as well."

He stood and gave me a hug. "I look forward to them. Thank you. You had a doctor's appointment today, right? How did it go?"

I wished he hadn't asked me that. I was trying my best to forget about Marcus and his little girlfriend. I kept wondering what she looked like. How often they were sleeping together, and if he did the things he did to me to her. I hated the thought of him being intimate with someone else.

"It was fine," I lied. "This little person is doing fine, and so is his mother. I was hoping to find out the sex, but the little guy or gal had their leg in the way. I'm think it's a boy, though, but I'll have to wait until the next ultrasound to have it confirmed. But it's fine."

"That's three fines, which, for a woman, usually means anything *but* that, but I'll move on. Sounds like someone is trying to make a surprise appearance. Marcus is a lucky guy."

"What makes you say that?"

"I'm 40, and I don't have any kids. I would like at least two, but I was dating a woman who can't have kids. Because I loved her I was willing to not have any or adopt. Now, it seems like all I did was waste my baby-making skills." He started pumping the air like he was banging somebody. I laughed. Jackson liked to make sexual innuendos from time to time.

"*Was?* You mean you and Alexis broke up?" He and Alexis seemed like the perfect couple. They were both smart, attractive, and worked in high-profile, well-paying professions. At least Alexis will be once she finishes med school. They had been together for at least three years.

"Unfortunately, yes. When she decided to go to med school, I had no idea the sacrifice we both would have to make. I think she forgot she had a man. I'm the type of man that likes to be catered to. I tried to ride it out, but I realized that it wasn't going to stop. She still has to do her residency, and she wants to work in a hospital. Hospitalists traditionally work long hours. I decided to get out now."

"Oh, that's awful. I'm sorry, Jackson. It's her loss. You're a great guy. Someone else will come along before you know it. Maybe you two can work it out. So, who is helping you celebrate your birthday tonight?"

"Not a soul. Alexis was planning something for me, but then she found out she had a conference to attend this week. Then we broke up. I guess I'll stay here and work."

He looked really sad. "No, sir. Your secretary is going to take you to dinner and a movie to celebrate your entrance into this world. In my condition, I really can't do too much more than that. The less moving I have to do, the better. You better not even think about turning me down."

Jackson's smile returned in an instant. "No worries, I'm not. I learned years ago when a beautiful woman wants to take you out, you let her."

I blushed. It was nice to hear that. Marcus barely even looked at me anymore.

Jackson noticed my reaction. "You may not see it, but you are glowing. You have been for weeks. There is nothing more gorgeous than a woman with child. I'd be honored to have you by my side tonight. Cute little waddle and all. So how about we both cut out of here about 4 p.m., and then I'll pick you up at your place around 6:30. Sound good?"

I nodded my head.

"Great. Now I'm headed to get my massage. I hope the therapist is cute. I might see if she'll let me massage her insides. I wonder if she gives penis massages." He exited his office and took off down the hall singing, "Happy birthday to me!"

I felt like it was my birthday. I got to leave work early and do something that I hoped would take my mind off Marcus. I was still mad at him, but I had to put that on the back burner for now. I had a job to do, and I learned years ago that only a fool lets love interfere with their money.

Jackson picked me up exactly when he said he would. He looked very handsome in dark slacks and a grey sweater. I had no idea what fragrance he was wearing, but I liked it. He picked a restaurant by my house that wasn't very crowded. Dinner was pleasant. We discussed some major projects going on in the office, and he also gave me some tips for studying to get my producer's license. I arranged for the waitstaff to come over and sing happy birthday to him. They brought him a large slice of cheesecake with a candle in it for dessert. He invited me to share it with him, which I did, and that's when the conversation took a different turn.

"All right, let's address the elephant in the room. How are things going with you and Marcus?" he said.

I let out a loud sigh. "There isn't a *me* and Marcus. Haven't you heard? He has a girlfriend. Her name is Chanel."

"I can't lie to you, I knew, but I promised myself that I would not get involved in whatever it is you two have going on. It's bad enough you broke company policy, but now there is evidence on the way that you broke company policy. I'm glad to see that you haven't confided in anyone in the office."

"Those gossiping heifers? Never. I don't trust any of them. The way they talked about Angelica when she found out that her husband was sleeping with Gina in accounting was a shame. Since most of them were Gina's friends they ganged up on Angie like *she* did something wrong, when it was Gina who was out of order. I saw firsthand that they could not be trusted. Sometime they would even keep Angie occupied so Gina could go spend time with her man. I don't discuss anything with them that isn't work related." I put another bite of the rich creamy dessert in my mouth. Mmmm. It was good. You could tell that the graham cracker crust was home-made.

"I always knew you were a smart woman. However, I have to be honest with you. Your performance has been lackluster lately. I know pregnancy can be hard on a woman's body and your situation with Marcus isn't helping. You've got to get your head back in the game. My father is quite serious about his no-fraternization policy. He couldn't fire Gina because Angelica's husband didn't work at the company, but he wanted to. Of course, he didn't have to after they were seen cussing each other out in the parking lot. They both fired themselves. We had a shareholders meeting that day, and the chair heard them. Dad was quite embarrassed by their unprofessionalism."

"I'll bet," I said.

"So, I must warn you, if it gets back to him, I will deny any knowledge of it. In return for not ratting me out, I'll do my best to protect you. Okay? But I can't go to bat for you if you're not producing. My dad knows great talent is hard to find."

"I'm sorry that Marcus and I put you in such an awkward position. I would never throw you under the bus. All I ask is that you give me the same courtesy. I know you and Marcus are boys. If I confide in you, what I say stays between us."

Jackson smiled. "Yeah, we met when we were both in the MBA program at MTSU. But between me and you, I think he's a fool. I've been watching you, Natalie, and I think you're a great catch. You'll probably make an amazing mother."

The tears began to well up in my eyes. His compliments were coming at a time when I really needed to hear them.

"Did I say something wrong?" he said.

"No. I've just been so emotional during this pregnancy, and that's the nicest thing anyone has said to me in a while. Marcus won't touch me. It's like I'm a leper since I got pregnant. Now, I find out he has a girlfriend. For months it was just us. It's like someone took my man, only he was never mine. I feel so alone. It's all just too much."

Jackson took the cloth napkin from his lap and wiped away my tears. "There, there, pretty lady. Marcus is doing the best he can under the circumstances. He stopped sleeping with you because he doesn't want to lead you on. He cares for you and has a great amount of respect for you as a person and as the mother of his child."

"I don't want his respect. I want his love."

"But I'm sure you don't want it under duress, do you? You deserve better than that, Natalie. You deserve a man who adores you. Not someone who kind of likes you because you're having his baby."

"You're right. This just isn't how I envisioned raising my child."

Jackson placed his hand on top of mine and held it loosely. "Of course not. You have to focus on the bigger picture. You are about to bring an amazing little person into the world. You are about to be a mother, and that is a reason to celebrate. You hurt Marcus today. He's wanted to be there for you and the baby, and you pushed him away. Don't let your personal feelings toward him keep you from allowing him to be the kind of father he wants to be."

I looked at him a little bewildered. "He told you about that? He should be talking to me, not you. Exactly what kind of father does he want to be?"

"One who is an active participant in his child's life. He is willing to give his time and his money to make sure that this little one you're carrying has a good life. Don't mess that up because the one who will really suffer is your child."

I sniffed and said, "You're right, but it hurts."

"I know it does, but hurting him isn't going to make it any better." Jackson smiled at me and somehow it made me feel a little bit better. He actually has an amazing smile. Jackson is more handsome than Marcus; he's pretty-boy-movie-star handsome and Marcus is more around the way boy-handsome. I never liked the pretty boys. The ones who were just a little rough around the edges or hadn't realized that they were attractive always got my attention.

"Enough of the tears. Let's get out of here," said Jackson. "How about we rent something and go back to your place instead of going to the theater?"

Was Jackson coming on to me? Surely he couldn't want to sleep with a pregnant woman. Especially one who was carrying his boy's baby.

As if he read my mind, he said, "I promise I won't try anything, but I just don't feel like being in a crowded theater tonight. I'll also be honest. I don't want to be alone on my birthday. If it's a little too much, I understand, but I thought I'd ask. I think we could both use a friend tonight."

He was right. I hadn't had a man sleep near me in almost a month. So what if it wasn't Marcus. He didn't want me anyway. I'd focus on the comfort that was being offered instead of the one I wanted.

Even though it was his birthday, Jackson paid for dinner, and then we drove to the nearest Redbox and picked out a movie. I'd like to be able to say the title of what we watched and what it was about, but I can't. The three of us—me, Jackson, and Pepper, were soundly asleep on the couch within the first 15 minutes. I enjoyed resting in his arms. I can't say that it felt right, but it didn't feel wrong either. The next morning, Jackson took me to breakfast and told me I could take my time coming in. He thanked me several times for helping him to take his mind off Alexis and giving him an enjoyable birthday. I could tell he was really disappointed that things didn't work out with her.

Before he dropped me off back at my apartment, he said, "Remember what I told you about Marcus. Let that man be a father to his child. There's a man out there who wants to love you, and he won't have to be manipulated to do it." He then gave me a soft slow kiss on the lips and rubbed my protruding belly. The baby moved. I guess he needed some comfort too. I was a little surprised by his gesture, but I decided to go with the flow and just said okay. After I entered my place, I sent Marcus a text containing an audio file of the baby's heartbeat I made and a picture of the ultrasound. I wasn't completely heartless, just pissed off. He had Jackson to thank for my generosity. I had a pretty good boss. It didn't hurt that he was sexy too.

On my way to work my brother called. I didn't really feel like talking, but I answered anyway. He probably just wanted to check on me. I must have sounded a crazy mess when I called him after I left Marcus standing in the parking lot at the doctor's office. I had to let Jessie know I was cool.

I said hello and the next words I heard were, "We took care of that fool, Nat. He can't see the error of his ways or anything else right now."

"Jessie, what are you talking about? Took care of who?" I said.

"Your baby daddy. He didn't know what hit him either. I punched him in one eye, and then Manny punched him in the other. It was beautiful."

I could hear Manny laughing hysterically in the background. "We knocked that fool out and left him lying there," he said sounding like a hyena.

I had to make sure I heard him correctly. "You did what? Why? Where?"

"You said you wished you could punch him in the face, so we did it for you. We got him while he was having his little morning jog. We was gon' do it at his house, but we saw him and ole girl come out together.

When he headed to the park for a little morning run we followed him. It was so perfect. It was early. There was hardly anybody in the park. We even made it look like a robbery. He had a couple hundred dollars in his wallet. I think I'll keep that for my troubles. We did it about an hour ago, and don't worry, we made sure he woke up before we left. Some other joggers were helping him off the ground when we left the scene."

I was distraught and in disbelief. "Why did you do that? I didn't ask for all that. All I wanted you to do was listen. I was venting, not telling you to beat him up!" I was screaming at the top of my lungs into the receiver.

"Lower your voice. My ears are sensitive. Listen, I'm a man of action. Naw, Nat. When some deadbeat hurts my sister the way he hurt you, a real man is gon' take care of that. He was so disrespectful about it, too. I warned him at your crib. I guess he thought I was jaw jacking. He's the one who got jacked. He deserved what he got. He'll probably be walking around looking like a raccoon for at least a couple of weeks. I bet ole girl won't think he's so cute now. She must really need a man, to date one who has a baby on the way with someone else. She ain't even all that cute. Bald-headed scallywag. Her hair was so short you'd have to roll it with rice. She had a big ole booty, though."

Manny let out another loud guffaw and said, "Yeah, we got him good, Nat, Nat. And his chick ain't got nothing on you."

I let out a deep sigh. "I really wished you hadn't done that, Jessie."

"What's done is done. Me and Manny are gon' go get us some breakfast, courtesy of that fool. You want something? What you want me to do with his wallet?"

"No, I already ate. Hold on to the wallet and give it to me later."

"Will do and you're welcome," said Jessie and hung up the phone.

I know my brother meant well, but he shouldn't have done that. Violence doesn't solve anything. I had to get to Marcus without looking suspicious. I needed to see for myself that he was all right. I figured I'd start by going to his place.

As I pulled up, Jackson was leaving his condo with a bag in his hand.

"Jackson, what are you doing here?"

"I don't know how to tell you this, but Marcus is in the hospital. He was beat up pretty bad while jogging in the park."

I pretended like I didn't know that. "Oh no. How bad is it? Have you seen him?"

"Yes. I drove him to the hospital and after they decided to keep him for observation, he sent me to his house to get some of his things. Marcus has two black eyes, a broken nose, a fractured eye socket, and a mild concussion where his head hit the ground. He looks like he was in a boxing match with Mike Tyson. The only thing missing is the bitten-off ear."

It was worse than I thought. "I have to see him, Jackson. I'll just follow you to the hospital."

"Natalie, I don't think that's a good idea," he said with a sympathetic look.

"Why?"

"Chanel is there with him."

Like that was going to keep me away. "I don't care," I said. "I'm going to see about my child's father." It's about time I met Miss Thang anyway. Now was as good a time as ever.

Chapter 12

MARCUS

The world can be a cold place at times. In those times, it's always good to have two things—a heater and a friend. Since I've moved to my new community, I stopped carrying my heater—9 millimeter—when I went for my morning run. I guess you can say that was a mistake. At least I had Jackson there to keep me sane because the last thing I needed in my life was a vengeful heart. There I was—in the ER due to an assault and robbery.

The only positive that I could take from the event was that there was no harm done to Chanel. She sometimes jogs with me, but she was on her period and decided to go home. I should have taken the ambulance, but I was able to muster up enough strength to make it back to my place. I decided to call Jackson, and he agreed to come get me. I also called Chanel. She was acting hysterical. The last thing I needed was a screaming woman in the ER with me. I tried to get her to stay at home, but she refused and said she would meet me there.

So, here is how it all unfolded. After the attack I was able to make my way back home.

I got some towels and applied pressure to my head. It was bleeding—not too bad, but I wanted it to stop. I sat down and waited for Jackson to arrive. He must have been close by because he was there in 10 minutes. He walked through the door and began to look around as if he was a crime scene investigator.

"I got here as fast I could. You all right, bro? What the hell happened?"

I grunted a little as I made my way to my feet. "I got jumped by two dudes in the park. I guess I just got caught slipping." I began to touch the swelling under one of my eyes. "It was weird, though."

"What do you mean?" Jackson asked.

I got closer to Jackson and began to whisper as if someone in the room could hear us. "It was like I recognized the voices. The voices seemed so familiar."

With a look of surprise, Jackson replied, "Is that so?"

"Yeah, man, but it could just be one of them things. Maybe I hit my head too damn hard on the concrete, and it messed up my hearing memory." I tried to add a little humor to the situation, but I knew this was no laughing matter.

"Well, let's get you to the hospital. We need to make sure you don't have any fractures to your skull."

I reached for my car keys and tossed them to Jackson. I knew the last thing he wanted was for me to leak any type of blood on his spotless interior. He was driving his black-on-black Audi, and he loved that car more than he loved life itself. As we walked past his car, I began to think about Natalie. His passenger-side window was down, and I noticed one of her favorite breakfast drinks in the cup holder. I guess her eating habits were beginning to rub off on Jackson and the office. When we approached my truck, I grimaced as I attempted to sit. I suddenly clutched my chest. *Damn,* I said to myself. *I might have a fractured rib as well.*

In my midst of trying to find some comfort I joked to Jackson, "Man, I haven't been this banged up since Mrs. Kennedy's class."

He laughed a bit as he replied, "Yeah. She was brutal. But, hey, it all paid off in the end. She helped produce two successful brothers."

I grimaced again as I replied, "Well, I don't see how the hell this situation will pay off."

Jackson rolled down the driver and passenger-side window. He lit up a Black & Mild cigar. "I'm just glad you're safe, my man. This could have went wide left—fast."

"I guess you're right." I turned down the radio as I felt a headache coming on. I wanted to minimize as much unnecessary noise as possible. "How did your birthday turn out? I'm sorry we didn't get a chance to kick it, but you know how it is. Did you and Alexis decide to have a makeup session?"

I knew Jackson was having a difficult time dealing with the separation. I really thought wedding bells were in their future. I guess there was no such thing as guarantees in life after all.

"You know me, Marcus . . . I'm handling it. As for my birthday, it was cool. Didn't do too much." He paused for a second, then continued. "Natalie arranged something at the office for me—it was nice, real nice."

The mention of Natalie's name put a damper on my mood. It wasn't a feeling of hate or anything like that, but rather a reminder of our situation a day earlier. "Well, at least she's being nice to someone," I muttered.

"I think you two just need to sit down and have a nice, loooong talk."

Rather than dismissing his intentions I just told Jackson, "Man, I'm in no mood to think, let alone talk about Natalie. She's in another place right now. Being that she knows about Chanel, I don't see how we'll ever be able to speak cordially again."

Taking a pull from his cigar, Jackson responded, "Marcus, about Natalie . . . There is something else I need—"

I had to cut him off. "Man, I'll give you the scoop another time. I just wanna rest my brain for a second."

Jackson nodded in acceptance of my decision. He and I didn't speak much the rest of the ride to the hospital. I attempted to doze off a couple of times, but he kept reminding me that it wouldn't be a great idea. He had the window rolled down, and the temperature was in the midforties. I guess that was his way of keeping me awake and keeping his cigar smoke from sticking to his clothes.

Jackson dropped me off at the entrance and then went to find a place to park. I must have looked a mess because the nurse had me bypass the triage process altogether and sent me straight to an examination room. Two minutes later, Chanel walked in. I was elated. There was a nurse trailing her saying, "Ma'am, you can't just walk past the desk. Give me a minute and I'll see if your friend is here."

"He's here because he's sitting right there," she said pointing at me. She was wearing some black leggings with one of my sports sweaters swallowing her frame. She even had my hat to match. I didn't know what it was, but there was something sexy about a lady who wore my sports jerseys or sweaters.

"She's with me," I advised the nurse.

Chanel began to look me over and asked the nurse, "Can we get him some more towels? Can't y'all see these are soaked with blood? Baby, are you just now being seen? Are you okay?"

She had a million questions. I didn't mind, though. I was happy to see her face.

She was like the sun peeping through a cloudy day. I grimaced a little as I eased my way to a lying position. I elevated the bed to sit upright. "It's not so bad now. It's just that my ribs or something hurts every time I sit this way." She helped me put on a hospital gown, but I left my jogging pants on. There was no way I was going to sit there with my behind out.

Another woman came in and introduced herself. She was there to do the intake process. I reached for my wallet to get my ID and insurance card and remembered that it was stolen during the robbery. I began to plead my case to the young woman. She was very courteous. She provided me with a bunch of numbers to call in order to retrieve some of my important information. As I sat down completing my paperwork, I positioned myself to view the television screen. I wanted to see if there were any similar occurrences in the area as it related to robberies. The next thing I needed to do was reach out to the authorities to report the incident. I knew they were probably gonna ask me why I left the scene, etc., but in my mind, it was better to be late than never.

Still holding my hand, Chanel replied, "I'm so tired of random punks thinking they can just do as they please. No respect or regard for life."

I felt my phone vibrate again. I didn't even bother to pick it up.

"Chanel—I'm glad you're here."

"Where else would I be?"

"I'm talking about more than just today. I'm more so speaking on my whole situation with Natalie."

She paused for a sec. She loosened her grip on my hand. She sighed as she replied, "That was one of the most difficult decisions of my life. For one, people think I'm crazy or desperate for being with you. Two, I can't share the news with one of my best friends, because y'all used to date. It's just a mess."

I smirked through my pain as I replied, "Yeah, this ain't your everyday simple love story."

She returned a smile and replied, "Nor did I think it would be." She sat back for a second before she asked, "Do you think all of this is happening to us because we're in the wrong? You know, some karma-type stuff?"

"Wrong? Karma? I don't think so. I think this is just some real-life shit, and we're just getting a dosage."

She then masked a perplexed look on her face. "I don't know, Marcus. For some reason, I could have sworn that it looked as if someone tried to key my car. But then again, it very well could have happened when I went to the store last night. Either way, I noticed it today."

"Not the Benzo," I replied.

The nurse walked back in to ask some more questions and stall time for the doctor. I told Chanel to cool off the nurse, no more attitude. I looked at Chanel and knew that she was biting her tongue. She looked cute when she had a little attitude. My phone began to vibrate again. I ignored it. Whoever it was would have to wait, just like I was waiting on this doctor. Then my mind began to drift. *Keyed cars and familiar voices . . . This all has to be just a coincidence,* I thought to myself.

When Jackson returned, Chanel was pressing a towel against the back of my head to keep some pressure on the wound. I was a little woozy, but cognizant. There was some swelling around both eyes, but they weren't swollen to the point where my vision was impaired. Chanel was still frantic over the situation. I felt the tension from the shaking in her arm as she had one draped over my shoulder. "I can't believe this is happening," she said. Man, I felt like a lucky guy to have someone like Chanel by my side.

"Sorry it took me so long. I had a business call I had to take, but I saw Chanel come in, so I knew you were in good hands," said Jackson.

I smiled at Chanel. I sure was. We all sat there for about 30 more minutes, and then the doctor came in and told me what he believed was wrong, but he wanted me to have some x-rays to make sure. Before some man in blue scrubs rolled me away I asked Jackson to go to my place and get some of my things. I was hoping that the storm was over, but then my phone vibrated again. I decided to look at it. It was a text from Natalie.

I HEARD ABOUT WHAT HAPPENED. PLEASE TELL ME WHICH HOSPITAL YOU'RE AT!!

I was hesitant to respond. How did she hear so quickly? Jackson must have told her. I was in no mood to deal with her. After all, I had Chanel there with me. Why was she so concerned? It was only the day before that she was forbidding me from experiencing one of our joys as parents. I then noticed that I had another unread message from her. I started to open it, but then we arrived at the X-ray area, so I decided I would respond to Natalie later, in addition to looking at the other missed calls and messages I received. For now, I needed to turn off my phone and deal with the drama at hand.

Chapter 13

NATALIE

I texted Marcus to ask which hospital he was in, but instead of waiting for a response, I just followed Jackson as he went to take Marcus his things. As we entered the emergency area of the hospital, he tried to get me to leave, but I wasn't hearing that. I needed to make sure Marcus was okay. This was partially my fault. I also needed to know if this situation was going to require some damage control. My brother was wrong, but he was still my brother. I would do whatever I had to do to protect him.

When we arrived, Marcus had already been assigned to a room. The nurse told us what floor he was on, but once we arrived to his floor, we were asked to sit in the waiting area while they got him situated. I could tell there was something Jackson wanted to get off his chest, but I wasn't in the mood for a heart-to-heart. We sat there quietly until he broke the silence.

"Look, Natalie . . . about last night, I was wrong for coming over to your place. You're carrying my boy's baby."

"Yeah, I know. This could get complicated, and neither of us wants that. The good thing is nothing happened. We were both feeling vulnerable and didn't want to be alone. That's it. How about we both forget it ever happened?"

Jackson shook his head. "No, I won't be forgetting it happened. It actually felt good having you in my arms, but it would probably be best if we don't mention it, especially to Marcus."

"I agree," I said.

We gave each other a warm hug and just as our bodies were separating, the nurse walked in.

"You can both come in now. He's in room 901," she said.

We walked into the room. The first thing I saw was a woman in Marcus's sweats and college hat I assumed was Chanel standing at his bedside. She looked at me and smiled nervously.

All of the muscles in my shoulders tensed, and I didn't smile back. I didn't say a word. I just stared at Marcus. He was avoiding eye contact. I opened my mouth to say something, but Jackson beat me to it.

"Hey, bro. How are you feeling?"

"I have a splitting headache. They gave me some pain pills and a mild sedative but neither of them seem to be doing much good. Good thing is I don't have a concussion."

"You've probably got a lot of adrenaline still running through you. Lie down and get comfortable. You'll be feeling better before you know it," said Jackson.

"That's good advice. We were just about to pray," said Chanel. "Why don't you two join us?"

"Sure," I said. "Prayer is definitely in order." We all gathered around Marcus's bed and bowed our heads. Then, Chanel began to pray.

"Dear Lord,

We ask that you bind every spirit in this room but the Holy Spirit. Let all animosities and anger subside and replace it with your love and understanding. We would like to say thank you for keeping Marcus safe today. We also ask for your healing mercy as he recovers from his injuries. We ask that all his tests come back with positive news and no surgeries are needed. We also ask that you keep him, Natalie, and their child in harmony as they prepare to become parents. We ask for a healthy, happy, intelligent child who knows that he is loved and adored by both parents. These and many other blessings we ask in your Son Jesus' name. Amen."

The rest of us said amen. Marcus was holding Chanel's hand. He squeezed it tightly and said, "Thank you, baby."

She smiled adoringly down at him. "You're more than welcome."

I wanted to throw up. Why did she feel the need to put our baby in her prayer? I didn't know if this chick was even saved. She could be praying some coded satanic prayer I knew nothing about. She needed to pray for herself. Marcus finally turned his attention toward me. "Hey, Natalie. How are you two feeling?"

"We're good. Just concerned about you, Daddy. I'm sorry about what happened, but I'm glad you're okay. Did you like the audio file I sent you?"

He looked confused for a minute then said, "Oh, I saw it but haven't had time to listen to it. I've been dealing with my injuries. I got it while I was running. My intention was to listen to it after I finished, but then I got attacked."

"I understand." I fished my phone out of my purse. "Why don't we listen to it now? It might make you feel better." I pulled up the audio file and then opened the picture of ultrasound I took and handed it to Marcus. I watched his face as he listened to the *thump thump* of the heart of his unborn child while staring at the beginning stages of his development. He was beaming. His bottom lip began to quiver a little, but then he bit it. It was a beautiful sight to behold.

"Thank you, Natalie. This is nice . . . very nice. I know keeping Chanel a secret was wrong, but I didn't know how to tell you. I never meant to hurt you. I'm so sorry."

I looked at Chanel. She was now turned around looking out the window as if she were trying to give us a little bit of privacy. She took off the hat and ran her hand over her short, natural hairstyle. My brother was right, again. She had about an inch more hair than Marcus, and it looked like they went to the same barber. I had to admit she was attractive, but she wasn't all that. I looked back at Marcus and began to cry. "I'm sorry. This baby has made me so emotional lately. When I heard you were hurt I had to come see about you. I don't know what I'd do if something happened to you, Marcus. I'm not happy about our situation, but I don't want to do this without you. I can't do this without you. I grew up without a father. I don't want that for our child."

Marcus sat up in the bed and stared at me with his two swollen black eyes, "Natalie, don't cry. I'm fine. It looks much worse than it is. I'm not going anywhere. I'm going to be here for you and our baby. But I need you to understand that Chanel isn't going anywhere either."

Jackson came up behind me and handed me two tissues. He began rubbing my shoulders in an effort to calm me. I dabbed my eyes. "Thank you, Jackson. I don't like it, but I'll deal with it. Why she wants to date a man with a baby on the way is beyond me, but I have more important things to worry about than her psychological issues."

Chanel turned around and gave me a sidelong glance and said, "You need to be focusing on your own issues. Why you would attempt to try to make a man love you who clearly doesn't is beyond me."

Jackson intervened. "Ladies, please be civil. We just finished praying, for God's sake. This isn't about you. It's about Marcus. He's had a rough day. Don't make it wor—" He cut off what I assumed was the last word of his statement and looked toward the door. His next words were. "Head's up, bro."

I followed his gaze to the doorway of the hospital room and watched three people file in. I recognized the first one as Marcus's mother, Mrs. Colbert. I assumed the gentleman behind her was his father and behind him was a woman I had only seen in pictures hidden in Marcus's dresser drawer. It was Lisa, Marcus's ex-girlfriend, and she was absolutely breathtaking. She looked like she was ready for a cover shoot with *Runway* magazine. Her pictures didn't do her justice. I saw why Marcus was so crazy about her. When he saw her, his face lit up like a child's on Christmas, and everyone in the room noticed. I looked around the room, which was now eerily quiet. Jackson looked stunned, Chanel was developing a major attitude, Mr. and Mrs. Colbert had a genuine look of concern, and Lisa smiled sweetly at her former beau and then rushed to his bedside and caressed his cheek. Marcus's mother smirked. I knew from talking to Marcus that she adored Lisa and took it quite hard when they broke up.

"Baby, oh my God. You look terrible. Are you okay?" Lisa asked.

Chanel cleared her throat and said, "Hello, Lisa. I hate for you to have to find out like this but you're touching on my man, and I need you to cease immediately."

The smile from Marcus's face left as quickly as it came. He grabbed Lisa's hand to stop her. Lisa put her hands up and took two steps back. "Bitch, I've known about you two for quite some time. My real friends were honest enough to tell me that my girl was dating the man I wanted to marry," she said. I could tell it was about to go down, and it probably would have if Mrs. Colbert hadn't said something before Chanel could respond.

"Son, the doctor gave me an update on your situation. Thank God they just took your wallet and not your life. Jesus certainly had his angels camped around you. You had your father and I worried sick. I called your cell phone, but our calls kept going straight to voice mail. Did I hear this young lady say you are her man and she was a friend of Lisa's? What in heaven's sake is going on?" Mrs. Colbert asked.

"Hey, Ma. Hey, Pop. Hey, Lisa. What are you doing here? How did you know I was here?" Marcus asked. He mustered up a smile, but I could tell he was worried about how things were about to go.

"One of the men who helped you off the ground is our church member's son. He's been going to our church for the past few months. If you came more often you would have known that. When he realized who you were, he called his mother who called me and after you didn't answer your phone, I started calling hospitals. The nice lady in the ER told me you were here, and I rushed right over. Lisa happened to be at my home having coffee with me when I got the call, and she insisted on coming with us. She's in town to see her mother. It's a shame your ex can come visit your mother and you can't."

"I was gonna call you later to let you know I was here. That's quite a shiner you have there. I hate to see what the other guy looked like, slugger," Lisa said. "Marcus, what you two are doing isn't cool, but now isn't the time to discuss it."

"Thanks. I agree," said Marcus. He looked over at Chanel who was giving Lisa dirty looks.

"Son, you look like the dickens. How do you feel?" Mr. Colbert asked. Mr. Colbert was a tall handsome man with a neatly trimmed salt and pepper beard. I could see where Marcus got his good looks from.

"Pop, I'm fine. Sorry you two had to rush down here like that. I cut my phone off when I was taking tests."

Mrs. Colbert walked over to the bedside and began fluffing the pillows behind Marcus's head. "I am your mother. It is my job to be concerned about my son. Lisa may be willing to hold her tongue, but I am not. Now answer my question, what's this about a girlfriend? I knew about you having a baby on the way, but you never said anything about a girlfriend. I've met your child's mother, but I have no idea who *she* is."

She looked at me, then at Chanel, and turned her attention back to her son. It was obvious that she wanted answers, and she wanted them now.

"What kind of sideshow circus are you running, son?" Mr. Colbert asked.

Marcus let out a loud sigh. "I might as well get this over with. Ma, Pop, I'd like to introduce you to my girlfriend, Chanel. And, Ma, you've already met Natalie. Pop, now you can meet her too."

"Montgomery, get me a chair. This boy is gon' bring my pressure to a boil. I see why you got beat up. The good Lord was trying to knock some sense into you." Mr. Colbert took a chair from the corner and brought it to his wife who promptly had a seat but never stopped talking. "What kind of man gets another woman pregnant and then gets a girlfriend *and* chooses one that is his ex-fiancée's friend?"

"Ma, she wasn't my fiancée. I never gave her the ring."

"But you were going to."

Chanel and Lisa's mouths dropped open.

"You bought me a ring?" said Lisa.

"You were going to ask her to marry you?" said Chanel.

"Yes to both of you," answered Mrs. Colbert. "Montgomery, evidently you did something wrong in teaching him about a man's responsibility and integrity. A man's first responsibility is to his family. What in the world has gotten into you, son? Your father has been with one woman his entire life, and he's the only man I've been with, but you, you, son, think you got to have all the coochie."

Everyone's eyes in the room got big except Mr. Colbert's. He seemed to be amused by his wife's choice of words. "Ma!" Marcus yelled.

"Don't you 'Ma' me. This is the devil's handiwork if I ever saw it. He's turned my son into a gigolo. There are three women in this room that you have stuck your penis in, and it's obvious you have no shame."

Just as she said that, a nurse came in to check on Marcus. His mother turned her attention to her. "Miss, do you need some sex? I'm sure my son here can accommodate you. He seems to think he has to have all the women in the world."

Jackson snickered. The petite Caucasian nurse turned beet red and said, "I see this is a bad time. I'll come back, and no, ma'am, I'm married, so I'm good on sexual relations." She then scurried out of the room.

I didn't think it was possible for Marcus to look any worse than he already did, but add the look of mortification on his face and the impossible was made possible.

She then turned her attention to me. Thankfully her voice softened. "How are you feeling, baby?"

"I'm fine, ma'am. Thanks for asking," I said.

"No thanks necessary, dear. You make sure you take good care of my first grandbaby, you hear. I'm looking forward to getting to know both of you. I know this can't be easy for you. My son appears to have LOST HIS DAMN MIND!" Her voice regained its previous volume and ferociousness.

"Pop, would you get her?" Marcus said, pleading with his father.

"No, son. She's right, and you know I can't do nothing with her when she gets like this." Mr. Colbert still had a smile on his face like he was enjoying the show.

"I'm going to fix everything," Mrs. Colbert said. She then focused her attention on Chanel. "Miss, I would like you to leave so I can talk to my son. This is a family matter."

"I'm not leaving. And why does she get to stay? She's not family," Chanel said pointing at Lisa.

"You can and you will. Lisa is like a daughter to me, and she *is* staying because *they* need to talk. She's upstate crying in a bottle of Merlot every night over my son, and he's here crying in between women's legs. They need to talk, and it is none of your business what they talk about." She and Chanel stared each other down for several seconds. Chanel was being quite defiant and didn't budge. She still had Marcus's hat in one hand as she put her other hand on her hip and rolled her eyes. Unfortunately, Mrs. Colbert wasn't done with her.

"Marcus, when did you start dating bald-headed women? I have never seen you with a woman with no hair. I got plenty of wigs at the house. You can let her borrow some if you like."

Lisa and I both laughed. Jackson attempted to swallow the laugh that threatened to escape his throat and headed for the door. I assumed he was going to do his laughing in the hallway. Chanel let out something that resembled a muffled scream and then said, "Marcus, are you going to let her talk to me like that?! A minute ago you were telling Natalie I wasn't going anywhere, but when your mother gets here, you go mute."

Marcus tried to man up, but it was futile. "Ma, would you please behave. Don't talk to Chanel like that. She's very special to me."

"So was that security blanket you carried around until you were 12. Eventually, you discarded that because it was a ridiculous thing for you to hold on to, and I'm sure you'll do the same with her after you come to your senses. I am not the one who needs to behave. You're still hurting, son. I know you better than you know yourself, and you think you can stop the pain with women. You and Lisa need to talk. It looks like you aren't going anywhere for a while, so now is ideal. The rest of us are leaving. Chanel, you are going home or wherever Marcus found you. Natalie, you will accompany me and my husband to the cafeteria so we can get to know you a little better. You are a part of our family now, and it's time we had a proper introduction to one another."

Chanel tried to stand her ground again. That girl sure was stubborn. "I'll leave when Marcus asks me to leave," she said and grabbed Marcus's hand from the side of the bed.

"Young lady, perhaps you didn't hear me. I am not concerned about what Marcus wants, and as far as you are concerned, you are, now, what do the kids say these days?—A non-muthafuckin' factor. You shouldn't even be a part of my son's life. It's just foolish for him to begin a relationship while he has a baby on the way with another woman." She then turned to her son, "Marcus, tell your little friend to leave."

Marcus was silent for a moment as if he had to think about it and then said, "Chanel, I'm sorry, but I think you should go. Please ignore my mother. She means well, but it appears that she has been watching too much reality TV and has developed a foul mouth. Baby, we'll talk later when there aren't so many people trying to run my life around. I'll call you after everyone is gone."

Chanel screamed, "If I leave this room, we are *over*, Marcus! You are supposed to stand up to her and tell your mother I'm staying!"

He let out another loud sigh. "Chanel, please don't do this. I truly care for you, but my mother is right. I need to clear the air with Lisa, Natalie, and you. It only makes sense to start with Lisa."

 Lisa had been standing there quietly the entire time. She really didn't have to say anything. Mrs. Colbert seemed to enjoy doing all the talking.

Chanel developed a look I knew all too well. It was the look of defeat and heartache. Without saying another word, she grabbed her purse, but as she went around the bed she threw Marcus's hat at him, and it hit him in the face. She then slammed the door as loudly as she could after she exited. The force was so great it felt like the room shook.

"Ouch," Marcus said.

Mr. Colbert helped his wife out of her chair. Once she was standing, he slapped her on the behind. "I love it when you get ornery like that." The old woman smiled and then kissed him on the lips. "Behave yourself, Montgomery. Besides, I learned it by watching you." She then placed her arm inside his, and they headed in my direction. Mr. Colbert extended me his other arm. "C'mon, young lady. Let me treat you two lovely women to a cup of coffee."

I smiled and looped my arm inside his and said, "Thank you, sir. I really could use one." I was happy that I was the woman being welcomed into the family and not the one who was asked to leave the room.

"Me, too," he said and smiled.

"Now, Lisa, you two talk, but let me give you a world of advice. Do not even think about reconciling with my son. He has too much going on right now. He's not good for you or anyone else. I suggest you both try to find some closure," Mrs. Colbert said.

"Thanks, Ma," Marcus said. "Tell me how you really feel. I appreciate the input, but I think we can take it from here."

"Don't you sass your mother, boy," Mr. Colbert said. "You're not too grown for me to take off my belt. She's right. We are going to have a long talk later. I didn't teach you to use women as receptacles for your emotional trash."

"Yes, sir," Marcus said looking like a reprimanded child.

I looked at Lisa again. No wonder Marcus didn't want me. I didn't even compare to that bronzed Barbie who was now placing sweet kisses all over my child's father's bruised and swollen face. The smile he wore showed that he didn't mind one bit. I had his baby. It was clear that she still had his heart. I can't believe he let her get away.

Chapter 14

MARCUS

Seeing Lisa again was an unexpected surprise, to say the least. When she first walked in, I thought that I was having some type of delusional side effect from the blow I took to the head. Then I realized that it was no apparition. She was real. Now there she was, standing right before me—just me and her all alone. For a split second, flashes of memory began to cloud my mind. *I'm over her,* I began to say to myself multiple times. I then clutched my hat; the one Chanel had thrown at me with enough force to leave a small pang across my left cheek. It kept hurting for several minutes.

Standing to my right, Lisa was looking out of the blinds as she said, "I guess I would be lying if I said I wasn't surprised." She closed them as she continued, "I always knew she had a thing for you, but I never knew you had a thing for her." She began to question me with her eyes. She was expecting an answer, but I didn't plan on jumping into that quicksand.

I never thought that I would be having this conversation with Lisa. Honestly, at that very moment, that was the least of my concerns. However, I knew that if this conversation didn't happen, there would be no way I could have been able to move past it.

I simply replied, "It just happened."

Still reading me with her eyes, she said, "Things like that don't *just happen,* Marcus. There has to be some type of history. Something had to already have been there."

Now there was no reason for me to be 100 percent honest. What was I gonna say? *Yeah, I've always found her attractive.* I don't think so. There was no way I was gonna fall into that trap.

"I'm being serious . . . It just happened."

Her facial expression led me to believe that my answer didn't fully sit well with her. "Look, I can read between the lines. I see there is no reason for me to dwell on the past. I already knew y'all was together, Marcus. You know word travels fast, even from thousands of miles away. Technology and gossip is a mutha-for-ya. I never knew you were going to propose to me."

"You didn't know because I didn't do it. You told me you were moving to Seattle before I had a chance to call and ask your father for your hand in marriage. If you knew about me and Chanel, what's up with the interrogation then?" I asked.

"No reason. Just wanted to see what type of response I would get."

She then began to fluff my pillow and eased it back behind my head. She had a sweet smell to her. For just an instant, an old feeling came over me. Our eyes locked for a second. I could tell that the moment was making both of us uncomfortable, but at the same time, it felt natural. I guess that was to be expected. I mean, this was the woman I was planning on spending the rest of my life with at one time. We dated five years.

"So, how are things in Seattle?" I asked.

"Business has been good."

"Dating anyone?"

"Wow. That was quick. Now, who is doing the interrogation?"

"I meant nothing by it. Just having conversation," I replied.

She leaned over to rub her hands across my face. The softness of her hands caressing my face was soothing to my swollen eye.

"Marcus, there is no reason to be hard with me. I know the way we left things wasn't the best. But from the looks of things, you were able to get over me real quick. I mean, a kid and another girlfriend? My God, it hasn't been a year yet."

I sighed. I wasn't going to tell her that Natalie was just a sexual rebound. I wasn't going to tell her that Chanel was the closest thing to her, so that's another reason why I pursued her. That wouldn't have been fair to either one of those women. The last thing I wanted to do was let Lisa know that she would always have a one-up over them. There was no way I was going to give her that kind of power over my life. Therefore, I didn't even respond to the question. I tried to change the conversation.

I chuckled a little as I said, "I can't believe my mother behaved that way today."

"Welp, she has always been a little firecracker. She cracks me up." Lisa spun around to face me as she asked, "Now, you don't have an issue with me visiting or speaking to your mom . . . do you?"

I'll be damned . . . another set-up question. If I answered yes, then I would be perceived as being an ass, especially if my mother found out. If I answered no, then in my mind, that would leave the door open for her to always be a thorn in the side of any of my relationships.

That assumption would be based on her relationship with my mother. So, I answered her question with a question. "How do you feel about it?"

"You know, when I first came to town, I had made up my mind that I wouldn't visit, especially after hearing about you and Chanel. But I said to myself that it would kind of be rude of me not to go see your mom. I mean, just because we are no longer together doesn't mean that I have to stop being nice to her."

I fell silent for a second. Then as if she was reading my mind Lisa said, "She'll get over it."

"Who will get over what?"

"Chanel. She will get over what happened today."

"How can you be so sure?"

"We were friends for years. Trust me. I just know."

Well, I'm glad she was so sure of herself. I was hoping that would be the case. If I was her, I probably would have walked away with no return. I felt bad that she had been treated that way. But, I knew the best thing for her was to leave at that moment. There was no need to complicate matters more than they had to be. As far as I was concerned, Natalie and Chanel knew where we all stood as far as who I was with and the responsibilities that I have.

"I hope you're right," I said.

"You really like her, don't you?"

"I do."

"Do you love her?"

I could tell she wanted to believe that our love couldn't be replaced so easily. I hesitated before answering the question. However, she had beaten me to the punch and replied, "Never mind, that's not fair. Don't answer that."

In another attempt to change the conversation I asked, "How is your mother?"

"Nice try, Marcus. I still love you. I really miss you too. It's almost like I'm missing a limb. I knew this would be hard, but I didn't know it would be this hard."

I couldn't believe what I was hearing. I didn't know how to respond to that at all. Again, there was some awkward silence between the two of us. Then she proceeded to hit me with the nail in the coffin. "Do you still love me, Marcus?"

Again, I had become mute. Before I was about to utter something that I would have to answer to for, presumably, the rest of my life, I was saved by the bell. The doctor walked in to check on me. I was relieved.

After having a brief dialogue with my doctor, Lisa grabbed her coat. "Well, it looks like you're in good hands now, Marcus. I promised my mother I'd take her to lunch. Please tell your parents good-bye for me." She then walked next to my bed and leaned over to give me a hug. She whispered, "For the record, you don't have to answer that question either. But I meant what I said. However, I also love you to the point to know when to walk away." She kissed me on my swollen face and proceeded to walk out the door. And just like that, she was gone. Was she gone for good, I didn't know, but at that moment, for just a split second, it felt like the day she had left for Seattle all over again.

***

I was beginning to feel a little better after the whole attacking ordeal I experienced. My hospital stay was short and sweet. I was glad to learn that I didn't suffer any long-term damages to the head. Both eyes are almost back to normal. The only aftereffect I have is at times there is a slight discomfort in my chest area. The doctor advised that the pain would work itself out within the next 6–8 weeks. I still suffer from headaches from time to time, but the doctor said those would subside as well.

Sitting alone in the dark, I had a lot of time to think over some things. Chanel and I have been on rocky terms. She was having a difficult time getting past the whole hospital debacle with my mother. I had a conversation with my mother letting her know that not only did she hurt Chanel, but she had hurt me as well. I couldn't believe I had to tell her that. That was the first time I had expressed any displeasure over her actions. But to be fair to her that was the first time that I can recall that she went overboard like that. I tried to tell Chanel not to take it personally, but she wasn't having it. Despite it all, she still agreed to come over to my place to talk some things out some more. I hadn't seen her in over a week.

I thought about Lisa, Natalie, and Chanel. Lisa and Chanel were both able to penetrate a part of me no other woman had, but I had to admit there was one area where Natalie had them both beat—the bedroom. I mean, it was good with Lisa, and although Chanel and I were still learning each other's likes and dislikes, it was pretty good too, but with Natalie sex was GREAT. I can't put my finger on it, but there was something about the way her body welcomed mine. It was a connection, a warmth, an orgasmic invitation . . . I don't know, but it was almost surreal. It only seemed to get better over time when, with other women, sex starts to become routine and mundane. Natalie went out of her way to make sure she was full of surprises. It was like she was reading some manual for how to drive a man wild. Good thing I required more than sexual stimulation or Chanel would have never had a chance. I hadn't had sex in a couple of weeks, and I hoped Chanel would be in the mood.

As I awaited her arrival, I attempted to set the mood. I had some smooth jams playing in the background. I even took it back old school and lit some candles. Red wine was her favorite, so I made sure that I had a bottle on deck. It was killing me on the inside not having her around.

I decided that I would go ahead and start working on that bottle of wine to make the time go faster, at least in my mind it would. I was having a nice little groove going. Next thing I knew, I found myself waking up after what seemed like a power nap. However, it ended up being later than I thought. I reached for my phone to check the time. It was a little past eleven. I began to panic. I know I didn't miss Chanel by oversleeping. I frantically checked for a text message and any missed calls—nothing. I darted to the window to see if her car was outside—nothing. *Damn, maybe she decided not to come after all.*

I waited for another 20 minutes or so before I decided to give her a call. As I was about to finish dialing the last couple of numbers, there was a knock on the door. I began to feel at ease. My baby was back. I couldn't wait to see and kiss her face. I couldn't wait to rub my hands through her natural hair. I couldn't wait to share a glass of wine with her. I couldn't wait to caress her body with my magical hands. I stopped dialing and was speaking aloud as I was approaching the door. "I thought you had forgotten all about . . ."

As I pulled the door open, I realized that it wasn't Chanel. It was the other woman in my life—Natalie.

Chapter 15

NATALIE

I don't know what made me just pop up at Marcus's house. It was probably loneliness. It's bad enough being pregnant, but being pregnant and alone is the pits. Jackson said I could call him anytime, but truth be told, Jackson was just a poor substitute for the man I really want. We hung out a couple more times. He even kissed me once, but we both decided to end it before things went too far. Besides, I wasn't like Marcus. I couldn't date friends with a clear conscience. It just felt so wrong whenever Jackson and I were together. But at least somebody wanted me.

I was leaving Marcus's parents' house when I made the detour to his. I'd been spending a lot of time talking to his mother since that fiasco at the hospital. I had a great time with his parents. They're really good people. I saw where Marcus got his wit and his intellect from. His mother may come up off a little feisty, but it's only because she is frustrated with the way Marcus is living his life. As she explained to me, "It's hard for a mother to see her son standing in front of a train and not want to do all you can to push him out of the way. My son is becoming a womanizer all because he has a broken heart. It's not healthy." She also said something else that got me to thinking. "Natalie, you may not be my son's type, but you and this baby may be just what he needs. He's always chased after the glamour when what he really needs is the grounded. Don't give up on him. Give him some time. He'll come around. I feel it in my bones."

I hoped she was right I thought after Marcus finished talking to Lisa he would want to talk to me, but he didn't. He said he just wanted to rest. . I just needed to see him. Marcus looked surprised when he opened the door. When I entered I could see why. The place was decorated with candles and rose petals. Luther Vandross was playing softly through his Bose sound system. I knew he didn't do all that for me. He never did any of that for me. The most romantic gesture I got was a bubble bath on my birthday. He looked delicious and the smell emanating from his body was something I'd never smelled on him. It had to be new and I liked it— a lot. All that must have been for Chanel. I didn't care. I had some things I had to get off my chest. Luther would just have to back me up.

"Hi," I said.

"Hey. Is everything okay?"

"Yeah. I'm okay, and he's okay. Can I get a hug?"

Marcus came toward me and gave the side-arm church hug. I wondered if he was trying not to squish the little one or if he just really didn't want to hug me. He hadn't touched me in weeks and my body was having serious withdrawals. "My bad, Natalie. I just wasn't expecting you. You still think it's going to be a boy."

"That's what I'm hoping for," I said while rubbing my belly. He moved.

"Why?"

"So, he can be just like you. I want him to have your eyes, your smile, and that can-do attitude. All the things I love about you, I want this little man to have. The world could use a few more good men."

"That's sweet, Nat, but you have some good qualities too."

"Thanks," I said and reached up and caressed his face. Man, he looked good standing there in jeans and a fitted Polo shirt. His face had gone down considerably. There was still a little bruising around his nose, and he had a small Band-Aid on it. I was still mad at my brother. After I left the hospital, I called and cussed him and Manny out. They had no right to do that to Marcus. I still felt partially responsible and I was glad he hadn't figured out that my brother and Manny were responsible because that would lead him to suspect my involvement.

"How do you feel?" I asked.

"Much better. I go back to work tomorrow. I was hiding out here all last week. I didn't want the people in my office to see me swollen and black and blue."

"I'm sure they miss you."

"I missed them. I was going stir-crazy in this house."

"You should have said something. Me and the little one would have come to keep you company."

"I really needed this time to myself. I have a lot on my mind. Some things I need to figure out. My life. Both our lives are about to change drastically. You understand?"

Finally, I just couldn't take it. I had to get answers to the burning questions that had been searing through my brain for months. I tried to figure it out on my own, but I couldn't. I had no other choice but to ask Marcus.

"Why don't you want me?" I blurted out.

"Excuse me?" said Marcus. "Where did that come from?"

"From me. You could see a future with Lisa, and now with Chanel and not me. Why? We have amazing chemistry, Marcus, and when we're together, we have fun. Why are you able to love them but not me? I mean, I *am* the mother of your child." I was fighting hard to hold back the tears. I knew if I started crying I wouldn't get an honest answer. He would tell me what he thought I needed to hear to feel better instead of telling me the truth I so sorely needed to hear.

Marcus let out a big sigh and began to rub the waves in the top of his head with both hands. He looked really pensive. It was as if he was deciding whether to tell me the truth. I stood there patiently waiting. I was going to get an answer. After about a minute, he said, "Do you really want to know?"

"Yes, baby. I need to know."

"You have no depth to you, Natalie. What you see is pretty much what you get. You're cute with a great body, but you have no ambition. You seem happy to work a job and watch reality TV. You don't care about social issues, politics, or the economy. It's all about fake housewives, women who were bedded by ballers and those R&B has beens who haven't had a hit in Lord knows when. I despise those shows. It's manufactured drama and dysfunction and it does nothing to benefit our community. Just mindless entertainment. There's so much more to life and how we can make an impact in the lives of others, and you don't seem to give a damn about any of it."

He was basically calling me shallow! I realized at that moment that the man standing before me—the man I screwed senseless for months—the man whose child I was about to bring in this world—didn't really know me at all.

"And you don't think what we have going on is dys-function? And it's the worst kind...dysfunction of the black family. That's the root of what's killing our com-munity, Marcus. And you, in your incessant need to find someone you deem is better than the woman bearing your child are contributing to it. If you want to impact a life, try starting with the two standing in front of you. We should be raising this child as a family and you're not even willing to try. You are such a hypocrite. You wear your "Black Lives Matter" T-shirt and shout "justice or else" at your rallies when it's evident that our lives don't matter. I think what you and Chanel are doing is injustice at its finest. The room suddenly became hot so I took off my jacket and laid it on the couch before fanning myself with my hands.

I was on the verge of yelling and I was exercising all the self-control I had not to. Marcus stood there quietly. I knew this was one of his business negotiation moves. Allow your opponent to become so upset that they are no longer thinking clearly and you can control the negotiations. If you're lucky they'll make a costly mistake that works in your benefit. I was getting upset and I willed myself to calm down.

"Would you like some water," he said politely.

"No, I need to get this out." I regained my compo-sure and continued with what I had to say.

"But the truth of the matter is you don't know me at all. Did you know that before I met you, I used to volunteer a couple of times a week at a shelter for battered women? I sat and listen to battered and bruised women pour out their hearts about the man who said he would protect them but only beat them and caused them to live in fear. Then, after we cried, I dried their tears and I tried to do something—anything—to cheer them up."

He looked at me like I was lying and said, "No. Why did you stop?"

"Because I met you. I was so attention deprived and lonely that I started devoting my time to you instead of them. Those women are the reason I got hooked on those shows. We would watch them together to get their minds off the fact that they and their children had no money, no home, and were often in hiding from their abuser.

"Did you know that I trade stock options?"

This time Marcus looked at me even more bewildered than before. "No."

"Well, I do, and I'm getting pretty darn good at it. Last month, I made $2,000." Marcus's mouth fell open. "Yep. I almost made my monthly salary in a matter of days. I didn't tell you because my mother always told me what's in your pocketbook is no man's business other than your husband's. Maybe I'm not at rallies asking for vigilante cops to be brought to justice, but I do care about social issues AND the economy. I am not just happy going to work every day, but until recently, I only saw that job as a job, but Jackson has showed me that it can be doorway to a very lucrative career. Furthermore, did it ever dawn on you that I would be interested in the things you are interested in if you bothered to share that aspect of your life with me? I'm good for more than sex and a friendly game of spades, Marcus. You were just too busy screwing me to notice."

Marcus started to say something, but I put up my hand signaling for him to shut up. "Look, I didn't come here to fight. I came here to ask you to truly give us a chance. Since I don't enjoy sex in my present condition, maybe this could be a good time to get to really know each other. I love you, Marcus, and it's tearing me up inside that you won't even try to love me back."

"Natalie, I never meant to hurt you. I care for you. I really do but—"

I cut him off with a kiss and then looked into those big beautiful brown eyes I loved so much and said... "Do you know how hard it is to see you with Chanel? How disrespected I feel? You couldn't have at least waited until the baby was born and a few months old before you moved on? You're going to make me do all those 2 a.m. and 4 a.m. feedings by myself? Do you really think Chanel is going to be okay with you being at my house all the time? You and I both know once he gets here, you won't be able to stay away. Not to mention the torture I'm going to feel having you around all the time and not being able to touch you."

He stared back at me with an intensity that made my body yearn for the physical connection we hadn't had in months. Then he quickly looked away, while saying, "I never really thought about it. I was just going to address each issue as it comes."

I took my hand and pushed his face back towards me. He was going to look at me while I was talking. "Well, I'm bringing the issue of us to the table. Marcus, I'm dying inside. Don't you even miss me a *little* bit? We spent months together. I miss you."

I slid as close to him as my protruding stomach would allow. I took him in my arms and started kissing on his neck in that place I knew always made him weak in the knees. He didn't try to stop me. Instead, he moaned slightly. I started playing with his nipples through the soft material of his Polo shirt. Marcus always loved when I did that.

"Natalie, of course I miss you but..." he whispered.

"Shhhhh," I said. "Don't talk; just feel. I need you, Marcus. This baby needs you. You have a choice. Choose us. We can be a family. Please."

Then, I resumed slowing kissing his neck. I wasn't too proud to beg. Not when my happiness and our child's was hanging in the balance. I wanted to raise him in a stable two-parent home. I removed my lips from his neck and put them on top of his. I kissed him slowly and deeply. I needed to somehow make him feel how much he meant to me. Tears began to slide down my face when he kissed me back. Our kiss grew stronger and deeper. My God! It felt wonderful. This man had no idea how crazy I was about him. I took my hands and began to undo his pants. I couldn't have sex with him, but I could definitely do something else he liked. I had pleasing him down to a science. While I worked his belt loose, I said, "Will you think about it, baby? There is so much about each other that we don't know because we didn't take the time to learn. Think about it, please."

After I freed Marcus's member, I rubbed it gently stroking the head and shaft. He moaned and said, "I'll think about it. Now, why exactly did you undo my pants?" He had that adorable mischievous grin of his plastered across his handsome face. That smile was like hypnosis to me. He could just about command me to do anything he wanted.

"Sit down and I'll show you," I said breathlessly. He obeyed instantly. I dropped to my knees, smiled at him, and then leaned forward.

"First Lisa and now her?" a voice behind us said. We both turned around to find a very seething Chanel. If looks could kill, we would have both been on the floor with the coroner on his way to get us.

Chapter 16

MARCUS

As if my life couldn't get any more complicated, I found myself yet again in a precarious situation. In my mind, I couldn't help but think that God was having too much fun meddling in my love life. However, I didn't find His sense of humor that amusing. There I was, sitting fully exposed with the soon-to-be mother of my child in between my legs. She hadn't gotten started, but I knew that wouldn't matter. I knew there was nothing I could say or do to help this situation. But I figured I had better do something quick or this could end up as a homicide case on *The First 48*. Natalie seated herself on the floor. I tucked myself back in, zipped up my pants and stood. The only words that came to my mind were, "Chanel—baby, just hear me out." Why did I say that? The look she shot toward me was unlike any other I've ever seen before.

"Marcus, you must think I'm one of these stupid-ass girls you deal with on an everyday basis." She began to approach me and Natalie with evil intent in her eyes. She stopped and as the tears began to flow she continued, "If this *bitch* was not pregnant, Marcus, I swear this would NOT be a happy ending for either one of you."

Natalie moved herself out of the way, and I slowly began to stand to my feet. The clinking of my belt was a reminder that I committed the ultimate disrespect. My once-stiff prowess was now limp in stature. With both hands up to express my calmness, I said, "Chanel, you have every right to be upset. I would be wrong to tell you to calm down."

She interrupted me and with pain still flowing through her voice, she said, "You damn right, you don't, Marcus!"

"I never meant for any of this to happen," I said.

With tears still flowing, she chuckled a little as she said, "And here I am, coming to you with open arms. Ready and willing to move past what happened last week. I'm such a damn fool. You know what, Marcus— *this* and you are *not* worth it. I'm better than this. I took a big chance on you. I lost one of my dearest friends because I thought a shot at what could be real happiness was worth it."

She then focused her attention on Natalie and said, "You can have him. I give up. But, please believe when I tell you this—he will never love your useless ass."

"Useless?" Natalie said while she attempted to wobble herself up from the floor to defend herself, but her body wouldn't allow her to move as fast as her mind intended. I then gestured for her to stay seated.

I knew I could have pleaded to Chanel to think things over. I truly didn't expect to see Natalie. I was indeed in love with Chanel —I think. I knew she was who I wanted to proceed with for the next phase of my life. However, deep down inside, I knew it couldn't happen. What Natalie had said earlier was correct. Things would never work with Chanel the way we both hoped. My situation was too complicated for her. Hell, it was too complicated for me. I no longer had a sense of comfort. No matter what I did, someone was going to get hurt—including myself.

In a somber tone I said, "Chanel." I slowly approached her. I reached for her hand, and she rejected it.

"I don't want to do this. I can't do this anymore. You're right. I'm not in a position to love anyone right now."

"So, you're telling me that we were a lie, Marcus?"

Natalie added her two cents. "Yeah, I guess it was."

I turned and with a little impatience in my tone I replied, "Natalie. Please. This has nothing to do with you, and you've done enough already, so please don't say another word right now."

I know it took everything in her power not to respond negatively, but I respected the fact that she held those feelings back and allowed me to handle this situation accordingly. At this point, Chanel was removing the necklace that I had purchased for her as a just-because gift.

"Something deep down in my gut told me it would be a mistake dealing with you, Marcus, but I figured the connection I *thought* we had would be enough. Evidently, I was wrong."

"You weren't wrong. *I* was wrong. I was wrong to get you mixed up in my fucked-up life."

With tears still flowing Chanel said, "We could have had something special, Marcus. I didn't care about your past or your situation with her. All I wanted and needed was you.*"*

As I was about to respond, she placed her finger up for me to remain silent. "No more words, Marcus. Please, don't call me. Lose my number, name, and address. I don't ever want to see or hear from you again."

I watched as she began her transition to fade out of my life. A distant memory is what she would become. A mere figment of my imagination is what I would recall of her. I hoped the hurt I felt would walk out the door with her. I didn't need any type of emotional hangover from this. I was sick to my stomach. As the door closed behind her, I began to look at the necklace that dangled over the arm of the couch where Chanel placed it. I proceeded to pick it up and balled it up in my hand.

Natalie was still there. She got off the floor and sat on the coach. She began patiently reading a magazine that had a celebrity breakup as the headline. Oh, the irony. No words exchanged between us. I didn't even ask her to leave. We just sat in silence. Two people, miles apart, but yet so close. Eventually, she realized that she didn't need to be there and left.

Chapter 17

NATALIE

I can't say that I'm not happy Chanel walked in. I needed her to get out of the way. My godmother told me to make him feel he needed me, but I could never do that with Chanel in Marcus's life. The time he used to give to me, he had begun to give to her. That was one hell of a night, though. If I wasn't pregnant I would have helped him finish that bottle of wine.

I also needed answers from Marcus. It hurt to know he thought so little of me. I'm a smart woman. I actually graduated third in my class in high school. I attended college, but after my mom died, I dropped out. I just couldn't focus. No, I didn't wear my brains on my sleeves. I actually started that behavior in high school when I learned that guys tended not to like girls that appeared to be smarter than them. But I never thought that it made me appear shallow. There was more to me than Marcus had ever bothered to discover. Now that Chanel was out of the picture, I could show him.

Her pain was the least of my concerns, but I didn't mean to cause Marcus pain in the process. I saw the look of hurt in his eyes as Chanel walked out the door. As we sat on his couch in silence, I wished I knew the words to say to ease his pain. I knew that pain. I felt it the moment I found out Chanel existed. I felt it again when I saw the way he looked at Lisa at the hospital. He gazed at her with adoration. I had never seen that look on his face when he looked at me.

When I got home, I took Pepper out to use the bathroom and after he finished his business, I put our pajamas on and got in bed. I took a deep breath and prayed:

Dear God,

Please make this right. My child deserves more. I deserve more. Please soften Marcus's heart. Allow him to let me into those spaces that I have never been allowed to enter. I know I haven't been the best Christian, and I'll do better, but I also want to be a good wife and mother. I know he's the man for me. I just need him to know that I'm the woman for him. If you could make time in your busy schedule to answer this request, I'd be extremely grateful.

Amen.

Chapter 18

MARCUS

A few weeks later, Natalie called to tell me she had some pains in her abdomen, and when she called her OBGYN's office, the nurse told her to come in. I knew I needed to be there in case it was serious. We hadn't talked about what happened that night at my apartment, and I wasn't ready to. I wasn't mad at her, but I was mad at myself. I knew there was a chance Chanel would still show up. I let the head between my legs think for me instead of the one between my ears. I didn't even make sure the door was locked! But I promised myself that I wouldn't make her pay for my mistake. We were talking, and I was actually enjoying our talks.

I felt like I was in the movie *Boomerang*. I always loved that movie, and I was definitely in Marcus Graham mode. I was at the point where he had lost one of the loves of his life. The actress in question was played by Halle Berry. Chanel was my Halle Berry. She was the one who had taken my mind off Lisa. She was the one who had made me become more ambitious with not only my career, but my life as well. She was the one who seemed to tame me. But, life is not a movie, and there would be no happy endings in my world as it related to my relationship with Chanel. I just tried my best not to think about her, and I honored her wishes and didn't try to contact her. I even deleted her from my social media accounts.

Neither Natalie nor I planned this. We knew what could happen, but we didn't take the proper precautions and now we have a child on the way. That's just the way it is. I began to really get to know Natalie. I was starting to see her as more than a sex object. The things she shared with me about the battered women's shelter and trading stock options intrigued me. Had I really read her all wrong? I guess that's why you can't judge a book by its cover. I guess you can say that we've become good friends. For instance, last night we were on the phone for *six hours*. I hadn't done that since maybe high school. Don't be mistaken, it wasn't a love thing. It was more like a final acceptance that she and I would be involved for the rest of our natural lives. We spent Thanksgiving with my parents. Everyone had a nice time. My parents love her. I must admit she fits into my family structure pretty well. She listened to my mother rant about everything and she laughed at my father's corny jokes. Her love for reality shows allowed her to form a bond my little sister because she likes them too. My sister actually listened when Natalie started talking to her about boys and the importance of not letting her love life interfere with school and getting into a good college. When my mom tried to tell her that it was like she was talking in a different language. Her boyfriend Trent was *everything*.

It's now nearing Christmas, and the entire city seemed to be in the holiday spirit. Bright lights and ornaments were at every turn, and cold, crisp Nashville air seemed to create the perfect atmosphere for a fat man in a sleigh to make his appearance. Not that I believed he existed, but since I had a kid on the way, I noticed all the

St. Nick propaganda being erected that beckoned parents to spend massive amounts of money.

I still had some lingering effects from the aftermath of Chanel's and my relationship. I was hurt, but not deterred. I knew that love would one day present itself at my doorstep, but I wasn't soliciting any vacant openings.

I continued to think about the turn my life had taken while we sat in the examination room waiting for her doctor. "Looks like someone is deep in thought," Natalie said with a drowsy tone. In addition to her pains, she had become less energized. She was drained emotionally and physically. I guess you can say I played a huge part on both fronts.

"*Who,* me? Not really. I'm just watching you rest."

"Marcus, I'm glad that you decided to come with me."

"The pleasure is mine. I shouldn't receive kudos for something I should do."

"Yeah, that's true, but to me, it means the world."

What have I done to deserve the accolades of *meaning the world* to someone—let alone three women? What did they see in me to hold me in such high regard? I searched for those qualities in my mind, but I was left answerless. Maybe this was God's way of slipping in some insight in the midst of his humor. Maybe what I considered to be blown opportunities were moments of clarity. The clarity I needed to fulfill some unknown destiny.

Natalie rolled over on her side as she slowly caressed her belly. She reached for my hand and placed it atop hers. She guided my hand in the circular direction that seemed to sooth her pain. She slowly began to remove her hand as mine became the sole provider of comfort.

This slight gesture was a reminder that my actions no longer affected just me, but this bundle of joy that awaited us. I refused to bring him or her into a world of confusion. We as a culture and a race have enough barriers to face. There was need to add fuel to the fire that was already within. I had just finished reading *Between The World And Me* by Ta-Nehisi Coates. He mentioned the lack of control over the black body. A black body primed to be taken from its owner. I again stared at Natalie as my hand continued to sooth our future prince or princess. At that moment, I made an internal vow to protect this black body. Better yet, I should say *these* black bodies.

Chapter 19

NATALIE

The last few weeks with Marcus had me wondering if that was what heaven felt like. He came by every day to check on me. He was kind and attentive. We spent a lot of time talking and getting to know each other. We even spent time with his family. They welcomed me in, and his parents' house began to feel like my second home. His little sister even began calling me her big sister.

I started having these sharp pains in my abdomen early this morning. They were spaced pretty far apart so I knew I wasn't in labor but when they didn't subside I called and made an appointment with my doctor.

I was grateful Marcus was there with me. I lay there with my eyes closed enjoying the soothing feeling of his touch. Marcus rubbing my stomach was nothing new. He often rubbed it and talked or read to our baby. It's beautiful the way he cares for us now that he's not distracted by another woman. I never want it to end. He assured me that the pains were probably nothing but I wasn't so sure and I hoped this visit to the doctor would put my mind at ease.

Doctor Sales came in and greeted us both. I quickly explained about the pains I was having.

"Let's see what's going on then," she said.

I was confident in her abilities. She had delivered the babies of several of my friends and they all raved about her. Marcus held my hand as she rubbed me down with that cold jelly they apply before doing an ultrasound. She looked at the screen for a few moments and then turned her head toward us. "Natalie, I need to call you an ambulance. We have to get you to a hospital right away. This baby is trying to come early, and we need to stop it."

"No, it's much too soon," I said. I looked up at Marcus. His eyes held fear that mirrored my own. But I knew his fear was a little different than mine.

"God, no!" I said.

I closed my eyes and said a silent prayer. I couldn't lose this baby because I knew if I did, I would lose Marcus too. I was finally getting everything I wanted, and it was all because of this little life growing inside me.

"It's gonna be okay. Natalie, I'm here, and I'm not going anywhere." He kissed me gently and said, "Our baby is going to be fine. We are *all* going to be fine." Then, he took another look at the screen. I followed his gaze. Neither of us really knew what we were looking at, but there was one thing that you couldn't help but notice.

"Is that a penis?" he said, pointing at a little nub protruding from our baby's body. The doctor nodded.

The corners of Marcus's lips turned upward into a smile, but it was quickly replaced with a look of determination I had only seen when he was discussing a difficult business deal. He squeezed my hand while gently kissing me on the forehead and said, "Just tell us what we need to do to save our son."

I loved this man and there was no way I was going to lose him. This baby had to be okay.

TO BE CONTINUED.........

Sneak Peek

NATALIE

After an entire month in the hospital I am being discharged. It took a while but the doctors finally got this little guys repeated efforts to enter the world under control. When I was admitted I was only six months and that is much too early to give birth. I was told that it might be caused by stress, and I had to agree to complete bed rest to get discharged. I readily agreed I was sick of this place. I was sick of being poked and prodded all times of the day and night. I was sick of bland food but most of all I missed my first baby, Pepper. Dogs aren't allowed in the hospital but Marcus snuck him in a couple of times to bring me some joy. Marcus has been amazing throughout my entire hospital stay. He, his family and my godmother made sure that I knew I wasn't alone. It's been a beautiful experience as far as hospital stays go.

I'm just glad the contractions are under control now. I don't really have any stress but what I do have is guilt. I feel horrible about what my little brother, Jessie, and my best friend Manny did to Marcus. He still has headaches and sometimes he even has nightmares that's he's being attached while jogging. I also feel slightly guilty about the role I played in getting rid of Marcus's ex-girlfriend Chanel. The night they broke up, I knew she was coming over. It was obvious. He had wine, soft music playing and rose petals all over the place. I wanted her to come in and see us together inappropriately. I used Marcus's care for me and his high libido as weapons to make it happen. I was wrong but I needed her out of the life of my future husband. My plan worked. She's gone and Marcus has been giving me and our child his full attention. The only problem is my conscience is eating me alive. Why couldn't I let go of the guilt? Especially since it was both of those actions that landed Marcus right by my side and I think he's almost to the point of giving us a try. He keeps using the words "us", "we" and "our". He hasn't officially made me his girlfriend but I know it's coming. I tried to get Jessie to let me tell Marcus what happened to give me some relief but he pointed out how much he had at stake. If Marcus decided to press charges Jessie could lose the endorsement deal he just got with Muscle Man Protein Powder and he's currently being considered for a role in a new independent film.

Jessie also told me that I could lose Marcus. I don't ever want that to happen. I'm in love with that man. Marcus is even moving me in with him so he can take care of us while I'm on bed rest. He didn't want me home alone, and he didn't want to have to keep traveling back and forth from my place to mine.

As I signed the last bit of discharge paperwork Marcus entered my hospital room to get me and take me to *our* house. I loved the way that sounded. He had been at my apartment getting some of my things to make *our* house seem more like home.

"He came in and gave me a quick peck on the lips. "You ready to go, baby."

Baby, I loved when he used terms of endearment. "Yup. I can't wait to get out of here," I said.

"Me and you both. I'll be much more comfortable at my place and I'm sure you will too. Sleeping on this hospital couch was killing my back. But before we go I need to ask you something."

I looked into those brown eyes of his adoringly and said. "Sure, Handsome. Ask me anything."

He reached into his jacket pocket and pulled something out, "What was this doing at your place?"

I looked down and in his hand was his wallet. The wallet Jesse and Manny stole the day they beat him up in the park and made it look like a robbery."

I looked at the wallet and I looked at him. I had suddenly went mute. I wanted to say something but the words wouldn't form. My chest felt tight and the room was spinning.

"I found it while I was going through some of your drawers looking for pajamas for you and Pepper. Is there something you want to tell me Natalie?"

I opened my mouth to tell him I had nothing to do with it. I wanted to tell him that Jesse and Manny acted on their own in retaliation for the pain he caused me when I found out about Chanel. Instead, what came out was a piercing scream in reaction to the excruciating pain shooting through my abdomen.

"Oh shit! I'm sorry Natalie. Calm down. I didn't mean to upset you," said Marcus.

I shot him a dirty look, reached over and pushed the button for the nurse. Someone responded quickly and said. "Yes, Ms. Tellis. How can I help you?" I had been there so long the entire staff knew my name.

"Call the doctor. I think I'm going into labor again! I screamed as another pain ripped through me.

Marcus stood there with a look of horror and shame on his face. He was there when the doctor said that I needed to try my best not to get upset. Was he trying to hurt our baby on purpose? Did he want answers so badly that he would jeopardize the life of our unborn child?

As the doctors and nurses rushed in I screamed "Get out! What the hell is wrong with you! I hate you! Get out!"

The doctor looked at both of us and said, "I don't know what's going on here. Mr. Colbert, but you are upsetting my patient and you need to leave."

Marcus didn't budge. One of the nurses who had become my friend, Nurse Brandy, walked toward him, got in his face and started backing him toward the door.

"I didn't mean to. It was an accident," he said. "I'm sorry. I can't leave. I need to know what's going on with my son."

The doctors put me back in the bed and reinserted an IV into my arm. A tear rolled out of my left eye as I realized that I wasn't being discharged from the hospital today. I hated this place but at that moment there was one thing or should I say person I hated me.

"I'll give you an update as soon as I can but for now you have to follow the doctor's orders and leave Marcus."

Marcus took one more step back which placed him outside the doorway and into the hall. Nurse Brandy then shut the door in his face.

I screamed as another painful contraction took hold of me.

"Natalie," said the doctor. "I don't think we're going to be able to stop it this time. You're about to go into labor. Do you want Marcus here?"

It was because of his stupid ass I was going into premature labor. "No! Keep him away from me. Call my godmother, Dr. Adina Frank. Her practice is nearby. That's the only person I want in the room with me."

I prayed silently. *God, I'm sorry for all I've done but please don't take it out on my child. Let me have a healthy baby please.*

Stay Connected

Keep up with the *Where Do We Go From Here* series at www.facebook.com/jmwheredowegofromhere.

About the Authors

JAE HENDERSON

Jae Henderson's writing exists to motivate others. She invites readers to join her on a most entertaining journey that imparts some sage wisdom and assists readers in further realizing that we may not be perfect, but we serve a perfect God. Now the author of five books, she began in 2011 with her debut inspirational romance novel, *Someday*. In 2012, she released the sequel, *Someday, Too*, and followed it with the finale to her trilogy, *Forever and a Day* in 2013. She followed those with two books of inspirational short stories, *Things Every Good Woman Should Know, Volume 1 and 2*.

Jae is a graduate of the University of Memphis where she earned a BA in communications and an MA in English. She is the former host and producer of *On Point*, a popular talk show geared toward youth and young adults. Other accomplishments have included serving as a contributing writer for the award-winning, syndicated *Tom Joyner Morning Show* and a successful career as a voice-over artist. Her signature voice has been heard in hundreds of commercials and even a couple of cartoons. When Jae isn't writing, she works as a public relations specialist. She currently resides in her hometown of Memphis, Tennessee.

MARIO D. KING

Mario D. King writes to change the world with works that will spark an educational revolution. He made his literary debut in 2013 with the release of his hip-hop novella, *The Crisis Before Midlife*. Met with rave reviews by readers, he decided to continue to encourage change in the community through literature with the release of his first nonfiction project, *What's Happening Brother: How to strategize in a system designed for you to fail*. In it, Mario provides a realistic discourse that embraces accountability and responsibility to systematically address the problems ailing the black community. Through his meticulous research, he explores solutions in education, entrepreneurship, leadership, community, and spirituality, amongst several other topics, to transform the thinking of black men and their respective counterparts. His love for the black family propelled him to embark on a different kind of journey with *Where Do We Go from Here?* King hopes that by helping to illustrate how misguided relationships can negatively affect the lives of all involved, people will make wiser decisions and strengthen black families.

Mario received his bachelor's degree in communications from the University of Tennessee at Chattanooga where he studied global culture and communication, psychology and sociology. He received his MBA from Kaplan University and will continue to stir up change and motivate those with whom he comes in contact. A native of Memphis, Tennessee, this husband and father of three now lives in Charlotte, North Carolina, where he continues to be a positive influence in his community.